Voices Without Parts
A Novel in 13 Stories

LLOYD REES

First published in the United Kingdom by Cambria Publishing.

Print ISBN 978-1-9164532-6-5

For Rachel, who has believed in me from the start
and who taught me to connect all the parts.

CONTENTS

FRIDAY'S MISSING FOOT

Symmetry is a singular phenomenon. It is the curse of ill planned city streets and jammed in terraced houses. It makes mockery of family photographs; it aches the hearts of astronomers and mathematicians; it causes crowds to sway and ducks in flight to arrow their craning necks in symbolism and symbiosis; it leads from Noah to Babel; it makes a pack of playing cards a biblical companion; it guides, goads and gods a million men.

But it's the one aspect of sexual attraction we can do nothing about. You can paint your nails, face, body, lips; you can flex your pecs, triceps, buttocks; you can flick or back comb your hair; flutter your eyelashes; wear silver, gold or topaz; strut, pout or blush, but you can't do a single thing about the unequal symmetry that foils these peacock, peahen acts. The same nature that abhors a vacuum all too often abhors true symmetry and, with cunning malice, narrows one nostril, shortens one leg, bows one breast or shrinks one testicle. True symmetry is a grail, but without some sense of an approximation to its parallelistic perfection we are maimed horrors. The one-eyed man is scarce ever king. The mastectomy patient is a hurt blank. The monoped is the modern leper.

So why did Man Friday, singleton, simpleton and unheeded labour force, leave that one unique tantalising footprint in the pristine driven sand? Where was his other foot? Was it so light that it brushed the powder surface like a breath? So leaden that it dug a pit at every step, a crater that filled and refuelled and denied itself with new fallen dust at each new stride?

It's a problem. But so is Heathcliffe's unexplained disappearance and reappearance three years later, gypsy-dark and hirsute with cash. Magwitch at least laboured hard and (quite) long for his money, though you may say he must have toiled fearful hard to raise as much as he must have in the ten years it takes for Pip to transmogrify into John Mills or Ethan Hawke. It's a problem when the cottages on Knightley's estate churn out unseasonal smoke in the gleeful height of strawberry picking, the apple blossom blooming anachronistically the while. It's a problem of some pedantic magnitude when a man rows single-handedly in an unprovisioned inflatable across the Mediterranean, up through the boisterous Bay of Biscay, into the churning Channel, over the cold North Sea to a haven in neutral Scandinavia. You may say Joseph Heller is taking the odd liberty, as well as his character, the oarsman Orr, this far. But you can't tell me Daniel Defoe was single-footedly taking such liberties with the lone, but limber-limbed ex-cannibal, Friday. No. Friday was comprised of the requisite number of lower limbs. It was one-eyed Robinson Crusoe who missed the mark, as well as the boat, when he spotted that tell-tale size twelve in the sand.

Let me tell you what really happened. It was a mild March day, though March means nothing in the Azores of course. Oh - forget your notions of some palm-fringed isle in the Pacific, this isn't Papeete. You can safely dispel your mid-blue lagoon too: this is not the place you imagined at all. You've probably got multicoloured cockatoos squawking in the upper branches of your imagination, haven't you? Almost certainly you thought you caught for a moment in your mind's eye a ring-tailed lemur disappearing through the rustling undergrowth that creeps right up to the golden fringe of sand, didn't you? Think again. Crusoe was an Atlantic adventurer. His name wasn't even Crusoe, or Selkirk either, it was Lopes, and he would hardly have embarked upon the tedious business of teaching Man Friday English, together with the doctrines of the reformed church, come to that, as a Portuguese monoglot and (fairly) devout Catholic. But then again we don't need to worry too much about geographical or nationalistic authenticity; we can imagine this story from an Englishman's point of view if you like. I'd have to be writing this in demotic Portuguese to capture the true resonances of Crusoe/Lopes' internal monologues anyway.

So, it's March 19th, not that the season matters much, the weather is mild, but it'll soon warm up, and Crusoe's tanned thighs are glistening against the cracked and frayed khaki of his cut-offs. His wild reddish brown beard will be another undergrowth scarcely penetrated by the hot arrows of the sun's flat, pale but burning disc. I'm afraid we can't have a lemur scurrying away at the approaching heavy tread of our hero because the ring-tailed variety originate in Malaysia, and they wouldn't have found their way to the Azores at this time, but there can be a weird whoop from high up in a baobab tree as a grey-black comically serious-faced monkey swings suddenly, impetuously from one branch to another. Sundry other cries, whether native to the isle or purely to Sunday night documentaries on BBC, can also be heard. The island is in fact alive with birds and rustles, but the beach is a thin deserted strand of fine grey-yellow shingle. It is still, save for the suck and scrunch of the lapping waves. The horizon is sixteen nautical miles distant, but to all intents and purposes a thousand miles away, and as straight as a rulered line. It serves to underline the featureless sky and mark it off from the flat, dark sea, which gradually blues itself in broad bands as it nears the land. There is no wisp of smoke, patently, because this is 1719, or even earlier if we go with Lopes, but neither is there a tiny dot or the top of a blue and white pennant, or even the wake of a 12 oared native bark. Man Friday cannot have been brought to the island by canoe, or sampan, or rough hewn catamaran. He must have swum, if indeed he is here at all. But there, as sudden as a Balinese sunset, or the gulp of a black edged letter on the morning mat, there in the sand is the unique print. A foot long and sharply indented at heel and toe-fringed end. We take in at first Crusoe's expression - wild-eyed and stern-nosed, a bronzed dirty face is caught full on our mental screen. Gingery eyebrows lower and narrow dark brown eyes to black hyphens. A tic in the cheek flickers a second. Then at last we roam down the eyebeams and focus on the object of our man's frozen stare. Imagine, if you will, a big toe on its own, divorced from its sibling toes. You may have to picture it protruding from the foot of a huge iron bedstead, a huge pink-brown stubby digit poking over the foot of the mattress. You may have to lower your imagined self to its level and purse your pink lips, as if prepared to take in this thick fleshy beast into your warm, moist mouth. Imagine all this and you have some idea of the enormity and physicality of the big toe that left its incomprehensible mark in that sand. It is a toe so massy it has delved into a million grains of desiccated rock and reduced crustaceans to dig a

3

mini-crater a half inch deep. By its side, and lighter but no less there, are four littler prints. Four minute Kilroy heads peering over the wall of your credulity and the belief system of a decade or more of solitude.

Imagine. Ten years of staring out at an empty grey-blue vista. Over three and a half thousand mornings of nothing more to look forward to than the next fish and the tedious sun, with only the hope that there would be a fish, and that it would be sun, not a driving, shelter-threatening storm. No one to talk to, no one with whom to share the idiocies of quotidian (and hourly) survival, no one to watch growing grey, more hairy and perhaps less compatible. Then suddenly, a human mark. The promise (and threat) of communion with another. But what a human mark! How large that footprint was, not to mention how singular! If even the impossible is allowed, reasoned Crusoe, could not the gods have sent a dainty size 4 (European) or 5½ (U.S.) to offer the mad hope of a female, or - dammit - a child?

There is only so long a man can maintain a fantasy that can support a regular erection and the subsequent bliss of self-release. In Crusoe's case it had been slightly longer than five months before he had even permitted himself to attend to the fantasy. It took him that long to overcome a natural antipathy to the thought of seminal deprivation and pollution. Then for a long time images of native women with pendulous mahogany breasts came, at first unbidden, then rather more reluctantly, to aid what he came to see as a fairly harmless form of self-embrace. After slightly over five years, the images began to fade and pall, and masturbation became a self-imposed duty of gratification. At last it became an insupportable chore. During this long time the visions were occasionally interrupted by other visions: of a serious-looking infant Jesus, or an even more serious-looking Jehovah, but their minatory expressions were easily dispelled, only to return in force when Crusoe briefly considered bestiality as the last option for a man of aching heart and wrist. Animal life on the island was limited to the uncatchable and the impenetrable, however. He had looked hard and long one morning at a passing albatross, but he understood that the mechanics of the chase alone were beyond him, let alone the difficulties of successful courtship and conjugation.

4

Thus it was, with five long years of celibacy weighing on his mind and his scrotum, that Crusoe's hopes were raised and dashed at a foot-gazing instant. It should be borne in mind, of course, that the sin which in a later century dare not name itself was less a sin at this time than an occupational hazard for those of a maritime disposition. Nevertheless, Crusoe was a god-fearing man and apprised of the dangers and darkness of the world inhabited by the sodomite and the catamite. He had once been approached in an overly friendly fashion by a curly haired cook aboard the *Santa Maria* and had felt the strange sensation of hair and toes curling simultaneously. This amazing juxtaposition had been enough for him to rebuff the putative advances in a very deep and gruffly hoarse accent. 'Nay, man,' he had found himself saying (in Portuguese), 'I take my biscuit and salt beef as any other man doth, who with pride may call himself a true man.'

In a way, of course, he'd been flattered. He was not a handsome man, and not even a whole man. Mendacious accusations of treason against the state in a Lisbon courtroom had resulted in the loss of two fingers and a jail sentence that had given him more than enough time for reflection on this latest addition to his bodily imperfections. Surprising, therefore, that the curly haired cook should have picked him out, especially when there was a young ensign aboard ship who had hair of the flaxenest, teeth like a new clavichord, and limbs like a young lamb's. All things considered, the cook's soft words had been the stuff to hearten a man, as well as darken a man's hopes for himself in this world or the next. But he had responded in his hoarse, gruff tones and that was that. At least for the following three months.

Then, in a coffee shop in Brazil, Crusoe had been taking his ease after a particularly strenuous coupling with a native girl in a room above the shanty store. The mulatto girl in question was still upstairs, preparing herself for the rest of the evening's clients, and Crusoe had been rather taken aback when the only other coffee drinker, an old man in a tar's loons and buff canvas waistcoat, came over and joined him at his rickety table.

'New to these infernal parts?' the man said.

5

Crusoe put down his pipe and scrutinised the stranger. 'Ay, it may be,' he said.

'They'll rob yer soon as look at yer,' the old man said. 'Look at this.' He extended one bony hand and Crusoe saw two gouged indentations above the knuckles of the third and fourth fingers. The weals formed small pale vees against the brown horny skin of the rest of the hand. 'Tried to saw 'em off,' the man added. 'But I was too sharp for their tricks.' Crusoe understood that the man's assailants must have been attempting to remove a large ruby ring and a thinner gold ring from his fingers. The jewellery was a startling accoutrement to the man's otherwise plain, but unexceptional appearance.

'Saw, eh?' Crusoe said darkly.

'God's truth. Rusty teeth too.'

For a moment Crusoe misunderstood and looked up at the man's face. His smile revealed a gapped and uneven row of yellowed canines and pre-molars.

'Could have died of the tetanus.'

Crusoe dropped his head to the hand before him on the table again. Then he dropped it still further as he felt the man's other hand fall softly on his lap. 'You're a jack, alright,' the old man said.

'If you mean I'm a man of the sea, that may well be,' Crusoe said, tensing a thigh muscle. 'But I'm a man for all that.'

'And fond of a piece of stale, I've no doubt?'

Crusoe emitted a deep, throaty sound, part grunt, part chuckle.

'I noted you coming down from the chamber above,' the man said, by way of explanation. 'But poor Rosa's a gangrenous piece of flesh, ain't she?'

'She's but a girl,' Crusoe started to say, but the old man interrupted him. 'She's got the pox, sure. You're better to go with your own kind in a case like this.'

6

At that the man's fingers moved against Crusoe's inner thigh.

'You'll unhand me, or regret it man,' Crusoe said loudly, and he pushed at the man's arm. It resisted for a second, then with screech of chair legs against the dusty boards, it fell away and the two men were a couple of feet apart. Crusoe was tensed for combat and half up on his feet, but the man gave an appeasing chuckle.

'No, man, don't be afeared, I mean naught by it,' he said. 'I took you wrong, that's all there is to be said.'

'Be certain you did,' Crusoe gasped, surprised at his own breathlessness. 'Them as did that to you were happen young boys, not villains, and bent on removing thy too straying fingers!'

'Mayhap you're right.'

Crusoe saw that the man's eyes were averted slightly, and it was this inadvertent flicker that saved him. He sprang to his feet and turned at the moment a large club came swinging through the air. It would have caught him roundly on the skull if he had not moved, but he caught the blow on the upper arm instead. His attacker was the sturdy matron who had served him his coffee, then disappeared into an inner room. With a lunge, Crusoe butted her full in the face, despite half being held back by his other arm as the old man tried to stop him moving. The woman's face opened with blood and she staggered back into a stone abutment from the wall behind her. Crusoe whipped back to her accomplice, but he had backed off with surprising alacrity.

'Nothing meant,' he cackled.

Crusoe wrested the club from the fallen woman's grasp and jabbed it at the man. 'Nay,' he said, 'You speak soothly when you call these parts infernal, and the folk hereabouts thieves and jackanapes, but if you value those fingers and those rings, you'd best be away with you.'

The man's eyes were drawn to the thumb and two fingers that gripped the club. 'I see by your finger stumps you're not such a stranger,' he said. And he made a sudden dart for the door and was gone. Crusoe laid the club down at the side of the woman, who was now hunched up with her hands clasped to her smashed nose. 'I'll call the coffee *gratis*,' he said, 'If that suits you, madam.'

It is doubtful if, after his long sojourn on the island, Crusoe was any longer as alert to danger as he had been in the coffee shop, and as he had once necessarily been in the harbourside streets of Liverpool and Rio de Janeiro. Ten years of listless security is bound to soften a man, make him sloppy and routine-deadened. Every morning he would stumble out of the ramshackle, palm wood and grass-thatched shelter he had erected, and had to re-erect after the various storms that had struck the island during the rainy season. Every morning he would stride fifty metres into the dark green undergrowth and disburden himself uncomfortably, largely as a result of his high fruit diet. Without thinking of the possibility of ever having being observed, he would take a broad palm leaf from a neat pile of about thirty at the foot of a particularly straight tree and cleanse himself. Then he would throw the leaf into a shallow pit where years of rotted toilet leaves embrowned and liquidised themselves into a dark rich mulch for the trees and thorny bushes that encircled his toilet dingle. Every morning he would amble back past his shelter and make for the fringe of palms that bent back from the beach in a woody windbreaking palisade. There he would pause and gaze out at the furthermost edge of the sea, where the waters darkened to gunmetal and almost black. Every morning he would sigh at that unbroken line, sometimes marvelling at the symmetry of the wind-blown wavetops curling like circumflexes on the sea's incomprehensible script; at other times depressed at the tepid flatness of the untroubled waters. Then he would wander down to the edge of the sea and walk in one direction or another, ostensibly looking for driftwood or jetsam, as a sign of a ship ever having sailed anywhere near his blighted paradise, but also out of a sense that walking itself was a positive pastime. He would find oyster shells and clam shells, shards of razor shell and tiny pieces of unidentifiable crustacean remains. This morning ambulation would last until the sun was high in the pale cloudless sky, but all Crusoe had to show for his ten years of beachcombing were a few interestingly shaped pieces of driftwood and an extensive shell collection. The finer examples decorated his shelter, but the remainder were discarded and now formed a crude shingle patio to the rear of his home. Since his own shipwreck not a single timber, rope, musket, pot or shred of canvas had floated in and nestled on the gentle shelving of the beach. And this was true of all the other coves, inlets and sandy stretches of the island's modest perimeter. It was as if Crusoe had been cast back to an existence before time, or whilst the Creator was still pondering how to people his creation with something subtler than the simple fish of the sea and fowl of the air.

But now, though he was whole and still fully ribbed, he knew he had a companion. He felt emptied of air behind those ribs, punched in the solar plexus by what he saw. That strange mark in the sand betokened another human being.

He spun round, his red beard pointing at the bushes behind him like a setter's muzzle. His sun-dazzled eyes winced as he scanned the green marbling for a swaying bough or a flattened clump of sand grass. His ears strained like a mariner's for a mermaid's sad song. His broad nostrils gaped and siphoned in the warm air of the beach for the scent of human being, though he had almost forgotten that pungent aroma. As he spun round, his hands had involuntarily raised themselves, as if to ward off a blow, and his six fingers and two thumbs formed a thick bead curtain for his vision in that moment. Dropping his arms as he took a step forward, he made a darting run to his left. He stopped and looked hurt, or alarmed, like a kitten after a fledgling that has unaccountably taken off. He moved forward again towards the undergrowth, still straining eyes, ears and nasal muscles. Then he made another darting run, this time to his right. A bird rose from the topmost branch of a baobab, complaining. Such commotion in the human world, it cawed to some far off mate.

Crusoe stood still. His ears were taut, as if on elastic, though he knew there was nothing behind him but the lap lap of the low tide. Then rational thought urged him with its need for explanations. He turned once more to the deep imprint in the sand and tentatively put his foot next to the indentation. It was two inches shorter. He hopped away and crouched down to take off his shoe, which was in fact a piece of once stout, but now ragged, sailcloth sewn into the shape of a sock with a precious length of the waxed twine he had recovered from his ship. Then he placed his naked, and surprisingly white, foot next to the print and pressed down hard, transferring all his weight onto that one leg. If the mark he left was of the same depth it would suggest two things: that the mark was fresh, and that its maker was a man of much the same frame and weight. If his own print was deeper, it would at least hint that the mark had been made some time earlier, for surely this interloper was a tall man, and at least as heavy as Crusoe.

The mark looked much the same, if slightly shorter. Crusoe was disappointed. In such a way do we measure ourselves and come at such disappointments, in terms of our difference from our peers as much as in terms of our commonality. Bending down and taking care not to disturb the original footprint. Crusoe wiped away his own barefoot print. He had used his left foot, to make comparison more easy, but it was almost as disturbing to see the two left feet, twinned like opening quotations marks, as the singleton imprint.

It was March 19th and a Friday, as far as Crusoe could reasonably reckon. He determined that he would name the day Good Friday, despite a sense of his own heresy. He did not keep a written diary, but he marked the passing of the days on pieces of flat wood which he kept in a corner of his shelter. He would heavily score round today's mark and celebrate the day, come what may, when 365 marks had tolled out another year on the island. If the enigma remained unsolved, he would at least have memorialised today's amazing event, and would not be able to doubt his own fantasising. It was a small resolution, but heavily pregnant with the humanity that lies deep within even the most solitary of men. The most devout hermit must wish his fellows well, be sanguine about their benevolent intentions, be glad of their existence, or things have come to a pretty pass, Crusoe thought. Nevertheless he had to let this consideration do battle with a number of rival musings as he retraced his steps back to his shelter. Firstly, there was the possibility that the mark had been inadvertently left by a member of a raiding party of fine and fierce young cannibals. But why should such marauding monsters take care to erase all signs of their presence on the island, and then overlook

10

this one huge clue? Secondly, and it was a darker thought again, Crusoe had to entertain the idea that he had turned stark mad. There was no mark. It was a mirage, such as he had heard of travellers encountering in the dry yellow wastes of Abyssinia. Another thought forced its way into his brain. Of course it was not a mirage, but had he made the mark himself? Perhaps on some sleepwalking escapade? But how could all trace of his somnolent, and perhaps dangerous, perambulations be wiped from his morning mind? He was too plain and sensible a man, he thought, to be troubled by black mares and go wandering from his bed in the depth of the still and soundless night. It must be a stranger's footprint after all. But could it be the mark of a man who might have been his saviour? Had a schooner sailed past his island the previous day somehow, when he was busy on some task inland? Had a longboat pulled into the shore, to cursorily look for life, and then retreat with a coconut or two and the news that the island was lush, but of little interest? But why only one sailor, with one leg, and one huge hop from boat to sand and back?

The problem of the missing foot has exercised many a scholar. Shakespeare, in verse that is solidly pentametric for all but the Porter's rough-hewn prose, tells us the tale of a Scottish king and his murderous wife, and he tells us in language that has its feet planted firmly on the ground of Renaissance verse. Then down drops Hecate from the tip of her moon and tells the foolish fiends that they dabble in matters beyond them. Every line is a full foot short. That's the bard for you, perhaps the punters at the Globe weren't too fussy, one might say. But then Gerard Manley Hopkins invents a curtal sonnet with more feet missing than a lawnmowed centipede. That's sprung rhythm for you, says Hopkins. You can't argue the point: both men have left their imprint on our literary heritage like the ploughed up sand of Bob Beaman leaping into history one fine day in 1968. Anyway, this pedalectomy is perhaps no great sin. As Hopkins remarked himself, "nor can foot feel, being shod."

But feet weren't always shod, not even in rough ex-sailcloth. And they're sensitive things, whether used for their normal pedestrian function or for more exotic purposes. Vicious sand ticks can get into those soft, vulnerable hidden places between the toes and tear at the flesh till it is red and raw. Crusoe knew this all too well. And it's not just this part of the foot that is prone to pain. A particularly ingenious torture of the sixteenth century was to coat a criminal's, or more often a political prisoner's, soles in thick sea salt and then sit back to enjoy the excruciating agony as a goat tethered to the victim's palliasse proceeded to lick off the salt, and several layers of epidermis in the rough-tongued process. And feet are sensitive too in terms of pleasure, it has to be said. One of the more intimate of the various joys of consensual foreplay is toe-sucking, apparently. Numerous examples of the ecstasies to be derived therefrom are recorded in works of the literary or filmic imagination, and on the pages of the tabloid press. Marcellus Wallace's wife's lover suffers severe back injuries as payment for his over-indulgence in the practice, according to John Travolta's character in *Pulp Fiction*. Most of us will recall Antonia de Sancha's equally enthusiastic indulgence helping bring about the demise of a certain cabinet minister from political power, and his subsequent descent into the dubious realms of sports journalism.

Perforce these were not the reflections exercising Robinson Crusoe as he sat, a full complement of toes tucked underneath his haunches, brooding in his sun-dappled shelter. However, there is only so much time one can spend on the task of trying to solve an insoluble problem, such as the origins of the large footprint in the otherwise pristine sand. Despite having nothing but time on his hands, Crusoe had to eventually give up pondering the question and return to a consideration of his quotidian chores. He scribed a circle round the date he had marked on his year-stone and fell to thinking about food.

He had a portion of fish left over from the previous evening's repast, but he was not tempted by it. He craved something other than fish and fruit. But there was no mammal life indigenous to the island, other than a small type of rodent he had seen scurrying away from his forages into the denser shrubbery. Unfortunately also, so far he had been unsuccessful in his repeated attempts to trap or kill any of the larger birds who shared his small kingdom. In his second year he had managed to lure a parrot into a cage that he had constructed from sticks and twine, but he had not had the heart to kill the creature. In truth he had rather feared the leathery hide and ancient sinews of the gnarled old bird, and he had decided to keep it as a pet instead. He taught it a dozen words, though it was rare that the parrot would consent to utter one or other of these gems from its precious hoard, and the raucous screech, when it came, could hardly be classed as discourse to encourage or console an anchorite. At odd moments it would squawk, "Damn your eyes!" or "God save us!" Sometimes it would call Crusoe by name, or almost by name, for it seemed to have difficulty with the rhotic 'r' sound. "Cue so!" it would say, like an irate doorman outside Harrods addressing an unruly crowd on the opening day of a January sale.

Crusoe nibbled at his fish portion unenthusiastically. He had smoked, rather than roasted it, over the dense white fumes of the previous evening's fire, a modest conflagration of sticks and leaves that were too green and damp for real heat. As well as meat, he yearned for bread, but there was no wheat, corn or maize on the island. He had experimented with the pale powdery seeds of a broad leafed grass that grew on the vertiginous sides of the island's one peak. He had pounded these seeds to a fine dust in a coconut shell mortar, using the smooth rounded end of the hasp of his knife as a pestle. He had been able to fashion a pale green dough, and he had fired it in his pride and joy, a homemade oven set in a pit he had dug in the earth which utilised six of the flat stones which he now used as Neanderthal calendars. The baking was successful but the bread was not. He had tried gnawing at the hard, slightly burned disc of grass seed, coconut milk and water but it made him feel sick. "Man cannot live by bread alone," he had said out loud that night to the blank dark heavens. Then, "But oh! If there were only bread!" The parrot had chosen this occasion to utter one of his imprecations, which Crusoe took to be a kind of rebuke. He did not repeat his attempts at bakery.

He turned to horticulture instead. He diligently tilled a small strip of land in order to establish a more orderly cultivation of vegetables, but there was scarcely any point, he knew. The smooth orange squash that grew on the island did so in abundance anyway, and his transplants did nothing to improve on this natural bounty. There were no other vegetables, just a prolific supply of bananas, mangoes, tamarinds, limes

13

and pineapples, plus other fruits which Crusoe had not encountered before, but took no great delight in. It was a surprisingly tropical fruit garden for a rocky outcrop in the Atlantic, you may construe, but so it was, or so it might have been. What can we do but believe it?

So, with mid-morning appetite scarcely appeased, but feeling a little less urgent about nourishing his lean, but not skeletal, frame, Crusoe allowed the thought of the mark in the sand to absorb him once more. The notion that the interloper, whoever he might be, could prove a danger to his secure routines had evaporated like the low mist over the shore this March morning. If he were only another castaway, there would be comfort. Two men could build a bigger and better shelter. Two men could perhaps work as a team and outwit one of the partridge-sized birds that nested in the highest trees. There would be flesh to cook, or smoke. Crusoe might even resurrect his earth and stone oven. There would be, above all, talk, if only in the lingua franca of sign language, if the new arrival were not an English (or Portuguese) speaker. There might even be games and joshing. Crusoe's feet, though shod in an elementary way, were considerably hardened by his years of survival on a bountiful, but sharp, island. He found it easy, and mildly diverting, to kick around one of the riper, more symmetrical squashes in a form of one-man football. His goal was a line of crisp seaweed and his game no more sophisticated than the practising of penalty kicks, but it was a pastime, and every man needs a hobby. He was quite good in fact, and could curve a ripe squash unerringly into the corner of the seaweed from twelve paces. So what if the new castaway was a monoped? He could serve very well as a diving goalkeeper. If he insisted on an outfield role he could at least get his head to the squash and help Crusoe perfect his inswinging corners.

Crusoe again considered the possibility that the owner of the footprint might well be a native, a black man, and probably therefore uncomprehending as to the sporting proclivities of more mature white races. How would Crusoe teach such an innocent the rules of the game? Luckily, the offside rule would not apply. But what if his opponent picked up the squash and ran with it, deeming footwork too arduous and impractical? Impossible, thought Crusoe, carrying the ball would not make it a viable sport.

Crusoe was not a modern man, though in some ways he might still be recognised today. Like some of our more unreconstructed males, he was capable of sudden acts of violence, like the thrashing he had given his coffee shop antagonists in Brazil. He took his pleasures from casual sex and football. He regarded both the culinary arts and the rigours of a healthy natural diet as painful impositions on an otherwise satisfyingly lazy existence. He had not time for spirituality, literature or art, and the cawing of the birds, the moaning of the wind and his own flatulence were music enough to his untrained ears. But he was a curious man. There were many questions which repeatedly visited him. He wondered about his own place in the order of things. He wondered about his own body - its strange resilience, its limitations and its stubborn regeneration of exhausted cells. He wondered also about its comparative hairlessness, his wild auburn mane and fierce beard excluded. Occasionally too he allowed his speculations to take on a more metaphysical hue. The phenomenon of laughter interested him, for example. He had little enough occasion to laugh on the island, of course, but when he did so - as once when he observed his parrot Simeon just as it stumbled off a low branch and fell fluttering and flustered to the floor - he fell to cogitating what it was that produced that rapid throaty barking sound in his own throat. No other of God's creatures could even smile, as far as he knew. He had been told by a certain Captain Jones that the seeming-laughter of the African apes was in fact the sound of agitation and fear, and that was the closest he had ever seen the animal kingdom come to any sign of merriment. So, men were unique in this odd capacity to feel pleasure at the embarrassment of others. But man was unique in feeling pain at the hurt of others too.

He wondered about this other gesture of humanity, crying. He was a hardy man and had rarely experienced even a dampening of the corner of the eye himself since childhood. Nevertheless he had known, and could recall, the fierce jerking pain of tears, and had certainly witnessed it in others, especially after a particularly moving and powerful act of coition, or an equally powerful thrashing by a master-at-arms aboard the *Santa Maria*. He was thinking of the young lad David, who had been too young to hide his unmanliness.

Would the company of another - even a man - ever make him laugh or cry again, he wondered. To be really unmanned was in fact to be forever committed to solitude, he let himself half-realise. The thought caused him to jump to his canvas-soled feet. He almost laughed as he ran back to the beach. What a fool he had been! Why could he not have thought to place a marker in the sand next to that sign of another's existence on his barren planet-island? If the new man saw a sign - a stick, a tiny cairn of pebbles, one of Crusoe's runic stone calendars - the stranger would know that he was not alone on the island. Once, in the early days, Crusoe had cried out to the wind, "This island's mine!" He had shouted the words in some jubilation. Now he called out again: "Only connect!" He felt a stab of pleasure at the brevity and pithiness of his utterance as he ran through the overhanging branches of the stunted trees near the shoreline. Without forethought, another ejaculation came from his lips: "Love is all around!" A startled chaffinch chirruped back and fluttered off to another branch. He felt the surging emotion pulsing through his six fingers and ten toes as he raced headlong and burst out into the bright yellow light of the beach. Then he slowed down, somehow sensing how ridiculous he must appear, and walked more steadily over to where the footprint had been.

It was gone. The sand was smooth and showed no indication of ever having been troubled by human hand, or foot.

**

When Lopes' bleached skeleton was found three years later, partly protruding from the white sand of a bland beach in the dazzling sun of a June morning, the Dutch mariner who had called his lieutenant's attention to the discovery pointed to the delicate bones of the left hand.

"He must have died in terrible despair," the lieutenant said. "Two fingers missing." He shook his head sadly. "He obviously had to gnaw at his own flesh to survive. That is too much for a man."

OF WOMEN AND RATS

"You say you can always smell a rat, but what if you were a rat yourself? Could you be so sure of detecting your kin through the odour of your fellows?"

Those were my new friend's words to me on the steps of La Barenceau, where we both had rooms.

"I have no nose, sir," I replied. "But I know flies in the milk, as our poet says."

My companion looked at me strangely. "No nose, you say?"

I laughed. "Please don't take me literally. You see that my eyes are separated from my mouth in the normal fashion. I mean, I do not share the same acute sense that blesses, or plagues, my confrères. For some reason, I have never been able to enjoy with the same relish that whiff of fresh bread baking that people tell me is such a delight. I can detect a vague aroma, but nothing more. But then again I am saved from the worst rancours of the fetid stench of dung in the streets, or the miseries of breathing in the body odour of a stale whore. Perhaps it is not such a terrible loss."

At that moment Madame Garnier opened the door to us herself, her young daughter Marie being indisposed with a bad chill, and the old matron's unique blend of garlicky breath and liberally dispensed lavender water settled on us like a low cloud. Even I, with my defective third sense, could detect those odours about my landlady's personage, though it must have been a far greater waft that invaded my friend's broad, sensitive nostrils

"Ah, Monsieur Lamor and Monsieur ... forgive me," she said. "I'm so bad with foreign names ... but I'm sure you grace my house." She was a vexing garrulous old fool and, I felt, uncertain of my new friend, despite his fashionable apparel and his renowned father's letters of introduction.

"You may call me Laertes," he said. "I have a confidence that you can manage those few syllables, Madame Garnier." He spoke an easy French tongue and was a man of no little charm, which he could display to maid and matron alike like a croupier fanning a new deck of cards. Madame Garnier smiled and wiped a frayed lace cuff against the tip of her copious nose.

"You do me an honour," she said.

We held no further discourse with her but fought our way through the garlic and lavender fug to repair to my rooms for a glass of sack. I was anxious to hear more about my friend's days at the Danish court. It was, naturally enough, the topic of conversation we had embarked upon almost immediately upon encountering each other at the rooms of M. Ducroix, our philosophy tutor, that morning. When we learned we were both lodged at Madame Garnier's we were filled with delight.

"You must visit us at Elsinore," my friend said, holding up his pewter mug with an approving air, having rolled round its aromas in his fine nostrils preparatory to imbibing. "We have but recently celebrated the marriage of good King Claudius to the widowed queen, but there will doubtless be further events to celebrate in the months to come."

I understood his meaning and I smiled, partly at his innuendo but also to show my gratitude at the offer. I had taken an immediate liking to his frank and playful disposition.

"And if you are as accomplished at the skills of the dance and the epée as your countrymen," he continued, "And I am sure you are, you will be the envy of us all. You will shine like the Northern Star."

"The North Star is a cold enough light," I replied. "If I come to your country you must promise me some means of warmth, I fear."

"We have maidens who will be all too eager to breathe fire into your loins," he responded without hesitation. "And we will take enow of this fine sack to warm your liver on the cold road, have no fears under that head, my dear Henri. But I mean to return as an honorary Frenchman as much as a Dane myself, at least in the arts of the foil."

It was an auspicious start to a friendship I wish could have endured longer than the poor short term we had, but I will come to that soon enough. It was most certain a friendship that one other party would have wished prolonged too. I speak of my poor sweet sister Eloise, who of course instantly fell in love with Laertes when she met him for the first time a month or so later.

From the moment he invited me to Elsinore I began to think I would suggest that first we should go together to Normandy when I next paid my family a visit. I should say that I had not been without a certain circumspection in this regard either, though hindsight colours such judgements, I know. My sister's honour was a matter of no small importance to me, and I was ever aware of her innocence in matters of the heart. Even the finest gentleman is still a man, and my sister was a very beautiful girl, as I know better than reportingly. Accordingly, it was not for some little while that I thought to mention going to Normandy, or even that I had a fair sister still living at home there. The candid and comfortable alliance we had struck up in our few weeks together, however, dictated it only natural that I should invite him to meet my honoured mother and father in due course. And of course it was unavoidable that he should make the acquaintance of my dear Eloise at that time too. So, when I could no longer put off the matter of spending a few days in the bosom of my birthground, I mentioned to Laertes that I intended leaving Paris and going home for a short while.

"Ah, how I envy you your situation, Lamor," he said. "Here I am, far removed from my father and sister, with precious little chance of seeing either for many a long month. But you are a mere day's ride from your loved ones."

"Indeed," I said. "But you have not mentioned your sister or father in such warm terms before. Tell me, are you very close to them?"

"My sister is the sweetest thing who ever lived," he said. "My father, well, he is a man to whom I owe much, of course."

"Not least the happy chance of our meeting at Ducroix's," I

19

interposed.

"*Au naturellement*," Laertes said, "But my father is what I would call a politic man, and sometimes policy and parenthood are uneasy bedfellows."

"What do you mean?" I said. Laertes, I had come to learn, was an honest man, but not usually this honest.

"I am here in France to study, that is most true, but I sometimes suspect that I am also here so that I am not there. In Denmark, I mean."

I made a bow, so that he would further explicate his meaning, but he seemed to think that he had said enough. Then he appeared to change his mind.

"Tell me, Lamor, these past few weeks have you had any dealings with a countryman of mine, a gentleman by the name of Reynaldo?" he said.

I told him an acquaintance of mine had recently run into a man of the very same name. A Dansker, my friend had called him.

"And did your friend mention my name at all, when he spoke of this rencontre?" Laertes pursued.

"Well, as a matter of fact, he did," I admitted. "But I told my acquaintance he must have the wrong man. This Reynaldo was asking after a disreputable countryman of his who was always to be seen the worse for drink in the gaming houses and in the dens off the Rue de Clichy."

Laertes smiled a bitter sort of grin. "Reynaldo is my father's man," he said slowly. "This business is my father's way of finding out how well, or ill, his money is spent on my education, I'll be bound."

"This cannot be," I said. "You are the soul of honour, Laertes. Or at least, the soul of discretion. What could a father be thinking of, laying such springes for the reputation of his only son?"

"I told you, he is a man of policy. This always would be his way. Let me show you something."

He jumped up and ran up to his third floor room, which was directly above my own quarters. I heard him stride across the wooden floor, and then I heard a different sort of creak, as if of the hinges of a travelling trunk. He reappeared at my side a few moments later, brandishing a parchment, his face flushed and fierce in the glow of the taper he held.

"Read," he commanded me.

The letter was signed 'Your loving father' and was written in the most garbled French I ever saw, but I managed to make out the sense of the contents with a stumble or two.

"Why," I said. "He here adjures you to a strict and moral life. What ails with that? He talks of missing you too." I read on, with some difficulty, for the script was thin, minuscule and hastily scratched, rather than written in good hand. "He talks about the queen's son. That is young Hamlet, I take it? And here, Ophelia, that is your treasured sister, I avow. He says she is smitten by the ragwort prince. Is that the word?"

He took the letter from me and read it out, pausing to correct a phrase or two of his father's faulty French:

Your sister blossoms like a jejune rose, but that ragwort prince infects her very being. He bullies her with tokens of his twisted love, that is to say his trenchant, overweening libidinous desire...

"Perchance it is only a father's natural fears for her innocence," I said.

"And as a brother I fear for that precious state too," Laertes said. "But I must suspect my father's motives too. Listen to this: *The King is afeared of the black boy, Laertes, but you should know I have a trick or two that will ensure my master's safety.* Do not you think there's trouble at the court? Perhaps my place is there, not here. But if there is something in the air why should Reynaldo be here in Paris, and not make his presence known to me?"

"Calm yourself," I said. "Why don't you come with me to Normandy and leave these fearful agitations? If it's true that Prince

21

Hamlet is struck by your fair sister, what harm can come of that? If your father feels he has the matter in hand, what cause for trepidation? Nay, I'll not give you leave to dispute, come with me, we'll away to my father's house and ride and hunt the boar, for the estate is plentiful in game. We'll sing good songs and not trouble us with policy."

Laertes set down his father's missive and, overcoming his initial reluctance he agreed to accompany me and come to the country for a few days. Our studies could attend our patience for that brief time, we concurred.

The following Friday we engaged horses and set off for my family home, Chateau Lamor, three leagues from Lisieux. We could have chosen to hire a chaise but I thought if we rode we could undertake the journey in a single day. My plan was to get as far as Evreux before the sun reached its zenith and allow the horses an hour's rest and ourselves some nourishment. And we were making good progress until Laertes' steed threw a shoe some thirty leagues into our journey.

"Tis a broken jade, this beast," Laertes cursed. "And fit only for the bone yard." He smacked the flank of his mount and I saw its eye flash with fear. In truth we had been riding hard on a rough road and there were specks of foamy sweat on the poor creature's hide.

"This is an unfortunate chance," I said, "But look, there is a plume of smoke just over that ridge. We will perhaps be able to obtain another mount for you there. There may even be a smithy nearby if that is a village and not just an isolated homestead."

We walked our horses towards the ridge and were immediately gratified when we saw that the thin column of smoke we had seen from a distance was in fact a healthy plume rising from the chimney of a tavern, and that there were several cottages clustered in the vicinity. Laertes seemed more hopeful that our journey might not be detained too long after all, for as he remarked, even this modest hamlet should be able to provide a blacksmith.

We asked at the tavern and were told that there was a forge not five hundred paces from that very spot. Laertes gave a young groom who was loitering outside the tavern a gold coin and the boy led his horse away.

"The beast should be restored to us in a fit state in an hour or so," Laertes told me.

I had already begun discourse with the matron of the place and I introduced my friend to her with some pride: "Madame, this fine young gentleman is from a far off country, and he craves a mug of your finest porter to restore his sense of the native bounties of our fair France."

"Whatever you say," the woman answered, and she poured him a tankard of ale. She was a gaunt, pockmarked old crone in truth, and my show of politeness was partly ironic, and thus intended to restore Laertes' sense of well-being, for I knew him to be of a changeable disposition.

"Here's for you, madame," he said, tossing a few sous on the grimy barrel top that served as a counter.

"Thank 'ee kindly, sir," she said, but without the slightest note of gratitude in her acid tones. Then, sensing perhaps that we were not best pleased by her meagre hospitality, she attempted some conversation.

"Tis far you ride, gentlemen?"

"As far as we may, when your smithy has shod my friend's horse," I replied. "In truth we are bound for Lisieux. I hail from Normandy, madame, as you may tell from my accent."

"I tell no such thing," she responded, surprisingly bitterly. "But I tell your compatriot is not from these parts. Is it Prussia you call home, sir?" she said to Laertes.

My friend examined her face as if it had burst into boils on the instant. "I come from the land of the Danes, madame, if it is ought to you."

"I thought it might be some such place," she said darkly. "They say the sun don't shine in such lands, save for Midsummer's Day. Would that be sooth now?"

"It is a damned lie," Laertes said, but with a cool reserve the words belied. "But for a day like today, with its pleasant Spring sun, it is true you might have to wait till June. But we are not blackamoors, or esquimaux, madame. We do not eat our own kind, or hide in furs like the bear, you know. I venture that we are not so different from the French, despite our colder clime."

"That's as may be," the crone said, "But I don't like foreigners. There, I'll be plain with you. They smell different to me. I'm sorry to say it, but our land is our land, and fit enough for them as was blessed to be born here mayhap, but not a place for them as is born in stranger lands."

I began to remonstrate with the woman for this. Laertes was a guest in France, I told her, and not to be treated in such an unseemly fashion.

"Forgive me," she said, "But there was a Danishman stopped by not two hours ago. He got my gander up with his talk and his tales and his uppitiness. You may be right, I suppose, I should not dress all men in the same jerkin."

Laertes took a sudden interest. "Who was this countryman of mine, old woman? Did he offer you loan of his name?"

"I wouldn't want loan of it, sir," she said hotly. "Damn foreign name it was. Sounded more like Portuguese than from the frozen lands, I'd say though."

"Was it Reynaldo, by chance?"

"Reynaldo?" I repeated, in some surprise.

'Something of that," the woman said, turning away. "Or Roberto, or some such nonsense."

At that moment, before she could satisfy our curiosity further, a young girl appeared through a curtain that led into another chamber. She was dressed in rude country clothes, a dress of calico and a crimson choker that looked as if it were a strip torn from a bandanna, but she was a vision of pulchritude such as I have never witnessed before.

"Madeleine," the old woman murmured, "See that the gentlemen here do not go without."

The girl blushed slightly and the flowers of warm blood that entered her cheeks were like June roses. Laertes seemed in deep thought as he drew me away to sit down on a settle near the door, but for the moment I was too taken by the sight of this creamy soft peasant girl to worry about Reynaldo, or why, if his business was in some way connected to Laertes, the man should be in this part of the world.

"Would you bring us a bottle of Rhenish?" I said to the girl, who was standing before us with her hands crossed over her lap not knowing what to say or do. "Or better still, a Burgundy. You have such, mistress...?"

"My name is Madeleine," she said. Her voice was as clear as a cow bell but soft and low as a muted viola.

"My dear Madeleine, I would be obliged for the Burgundy, and perhaps some cheese and bread? I must say, the air hereabouts seems to do wonders for the complexion, but just in case it is your country diet that is responsible, I wish to indulge."

She bowed curtly, revealing just enough of her peachy charms to cause me to stir with excitement. I could not desist from reaching out and grasping her hand. "And I have spirit enow to indulge my fancy," I said, "And coin, I might add."

She gave a flicker of a smile as she unslipped her hand and retreated through the sacking which curtained off the next room.

"What do you think?" I said to Laertes.

"I think he is a politician, like my father," he said gloomily.

"Nay, man, I speak not of your Reynaldo, but of the maid."

Laertes looked blank.

I smiled. "You say this fellow haunts you like a ghost, and I believe it, but you look like you have but lately come from the churchyard yourself, man. Be of cheer, for here is matter more substantial. Did you see the bubs on this serving girl? And I never saw such hair: it is the colour of straw with the texture of silk."

25

"She may be fresh in years," Laertes said, "But she is a stale, I trow. Did you smell bedding straw on her, I wonder, that you talk of her as you do?"

In truth I think I might have caught something of the whiff of the barn as I leaned towards her to catch her trailing fingers, but we were in the country and that was as it should be. Our Paris maidens smell of civet, and what is that but the entrails of wild cat? At least the animal odour that but faintly invaded my nostrils was that of the milking cow or the swine bred for ham. I did not choose to dispute it with such a taciturn companion, but I felt that these aromas were lightened by the scents of the hedgerow and cottage garden too. When Madeleine came back, I took a deep breath of her bucolic musk as she bent forward to set down our wine and two earthen stoops. Feeling her full strawberry locks accidentally brushing against my cheek, I said "How old are you, my pretty one?"

"I am fifteen at Lammastide," she said, in her delightful Northern French.

I was much gratified. But not as much as I was when the boy who had taken Laertes' horse returned sheepishly to announce that the poor creature was, sadly sirs, lame. There was a horse, the boy's father's, that we could borrow for a few days, the boy told us, but it was not to be had at this time. His father had gone to a nearby market for the day and was not due to return till nightfall. Laertes was indeed disconsolate, but it did not take me too long to persuade him that we were now bound to stay at the tavern for the night. We would set off at first light next day with my horse completely fresh and a new mare for Laertes. For now, there was nothing to do but take our ease and engage rooms from the gaunt old woman. Laertes tried not to look too much in the sulks, but he said nothing. He did not look much happier when we learned that there was but a single free room at the inn.

"You take it," he said. "I'll sleep in the hay loft that adjoins us. But you must promise me a decent bed at your father's house tomorrow night. With lawn sheets, I trust."

Normally I would have insisted on sharing the bed, or drawing lots for it at least, but I had other plans for the night. I think Laertes must have realised it too, for he smiled enigmatically when I started yawning not long after dusk, and declaring that the morning would come soon enough, and that I was for my bed.

We had spent the afternoon on a stroll round the hamlet, which was little more than the few cottages we had seen from the ridge, bisected by a dusty track. After that we had obtained a greasy pack of playing cards from the madame and entertained ourselves at piquet for an hour or so before a meal of tripes and spring cabbage. It was plain enough fare, but a passable bottle of sack helped our digestion.

Madeleine had served our repast and I had whispered a few words in her ear as she attended us. I had hoped it might serve, for I desired not to appear too bold in the presence of two or three hands who were taking a tumbler of ale after their day's labours. They were looking at me with that suspicious eye that country folk have for townspeople, and that you sometimes see in the expression of the lower orders when they encounter a member of the better classes. Indeed, as one surly fellow glanced across at me, I could not help being reminded of the flashing yellow-eyed glare of Laertes' horse that morning, when its rider had vented his anger on the beast's flesh. I was right to believe that my few honeyed words to Madeleine would serve, however. She came to me that night bearing a taper, as if she were on an errand to bring light to my chamber, and in all candour she did light up my dull evening in course of the next two hours. Perchance I should pass over the details of our pleasant sojourn but suffice it to say I tupped her thrice in that short time. And a better ride I never had, nor was there ever a more responsive filly that bucked at the touch of the bit than that frisky maid. It made me doubt her a maid after all as I lay back in my cot, quite spent, but I was well pleased at the day's returns, despite our delay.

Of course, I was subjected to some manly jesting the following morning, as Laertes and I saddled up for the latter part of our journey. The boy had brought round the promised mare by first light, and, a good enough beast it was too. This meant that Laertes was kind enough to wake me with the cock still crowing and the fresh tang of a new broken

27

day strong in the air. Even as I started to stir he made certain pointed queries as to my fitness for the day's long ride. I confessed that I had not spent the whole night at rest, but I said I was probably all the more rested and refreshed for my pleasant exercise nonetheless.

Later that evening, however, when we arrived at Chateau Lamor and when I saw the flush on my sister's cheek as she welcomed our handsome young guest, I had cause to think again about my openness regarding my little adventure. Her fuchsia pink tinge reminded me uncomfortably of the healthy glow on Madeleine's face at the height of our exertions the previous evening. There was no time for conversation before dinner, however, and over our hearty meal of sea trout, wild boar and bourdelots Eloise was fittingly quiet and demure, rarely raising her head from her lap except when addressed by her mother about some domestic concern or other. Even such asides were quite rare, in deference to my father's questions about my studies in Paris and, after the little satisfaction I could offer him under that head, some discourse on the state of the court in Denmark. Laertes was more animated than I had seen him for some time as he sallied forth on an account of recent events at Elsinore, and then, when my mother managed to steer him away from politics to family matters, as he wandered off into a paean to the beauty of his sister Ophelia,. I did notice that Eloise looked up as Laertes talked about Ophelia, but she averted her eyes when she saw me looking at her. My father was less interested in Laertes' filial pleasantries, however, and he contrived to rein the talk round to matters of state once again. Then he surprised us all by saying, "One of my tenants reported that there was a countryman of yours, good Laertes, at Lisieux yestere'en. Now that is something of a coincidence, do you not think?"

I reminded Laertes that Lisieux was the village we had passed through as we had neared our destination that afternoon, but he seemed not to be listening. It was as if a heavy arras had been dropped down before his face, for his eyes were emotionless and his features quite still. "Did this gentleman ask after me, sir, I wonder?" he said.

"I am not certain," my father replied. "Did you advertise your travel plans, sir, in case you might be sought after?" My father sounded as if he disapproved of such a course.

"Indeed not, sir," Laertes said. "That is why it is all the more strange that this man, if it is he who I think it must be, haunts me so. He follows me in advance, as if to say."

I remembered that I had told old Madame Garnier that we would be away from the city for a few days. I must have mentioned our destination too, I realised. If our precursor were indeed Reynaldo, he could have visited our rooms, spoken to Mme Garnier, and still arrived at Lisieux the previous evening, while we were all the while held up at the little hamlet on the road to Evreux. I felt bound to admit that it was I who had spoken about our plans to come to Normandy for the weekend. "But what is it that prompts this Reynaldo's haste to contact you, Laertes," I added, "When he has studiously avoided announcing himself heretofore?"

"I smell a mystery," my father intervened. "But I will ask my fellows to watch out for this messenger, if that he be, and I trust all will be resolved forthwith."

Nothing further was said about the matter, and Laertes seemed not to have it in his mind over the next two days, which we spent at leisure and at horse. Indeed, he seemed in good spirits when we met after luncheon to ride out on the Saturday, and in positively amiable temper when I suggested the following day that we ride out after mass to see the full extent of my father's plantains. Our estate includes a cool wooded valley between woods of beech and pine and we paused for a while to allow our horses to graze. As we strolled through a copse that was heavily scented by wild garlic and marjoram, we talked about the days of our youth. Laertes the while absent-mindedly picked bluebells and fashioned them into a rough sort of posy. "Why, man," I was forced to say, "You are of bucolic temperament after all. I took you for a man of city ways." He smiled at me and said nothing.

We returned to the house by mid afternoon and I was glad when Laertes begged permission to spend an improving hour or so in our library, for it enabled me to repair to my chamber and use the occasion for some much needed sleep. I knew enough of my friend's sober and studious disposition, but I trow my father would have been well impressed by it too, if he had not been taking a nap himself in the great room at the time.

Just how sober were Laertes' intentions was made clearer to me when I descended from my chamber an hour or so before dinner. I went out to the stables to have some words with one of our grooms and therefore I was coming in to the house by a rear entrance. Just as I was taking off my muddied boots, I saw Eloise hurrying down the passage from the direction of the library. Her hair was in a certain disarray, her eyes were akimbo and there was a wild strawberry hue on her girlish cheeks.

"Eloise," I called out. "Whither so fast, fair sister?"

She was clutching a volume of Père Augustin's *Sermons* but her startled expression did not betoken that she had been at her studies in some window seat with that sere brown tome.

"Oh, Henri," she gasped, "You took me quite aback! What are you doing here?"

"I could ask you the same question, Eloise," I said. "But it is nearly time for dinner. Have you seen Laertes, perchance?"

"Erm, I think he may be taking a turn about the orchard. Should I send Charles to summon him?"

"No, I'll get him myself," I said.

She offered me a quick curtsy and sped away while I made my way round to the orchard. It was a matter of moments before I discovered my friend. He was standing by an apple tree gazing into space as if waiting for some angel to descend.

"By my troth, Laertes," I greeted him. "You look as if have seen a ghost." He was indeed pale as a lace handkerchief and he seemed startled at my approach. "It lacks but a quarter of the hour till we dine, my friend. You must come in, you know."

"Indeed," he said, his voice like wood.

"What ails you, man?" I said, with some solicitude.

"Nought, Lamor. I was merely thinking how my life has changed these past few months and ... well ... of other things. I am myself again now though."

After dinner I succeeded in engaging him in intimate conversation once more, but not before our steward Barnard had handed him a note. Laertes was alone in the inner hall and just putting up the letter when I approached him.

"Is it some missive from the mysterious Reynaldo?" I said.

He nodded and gave out a great sigh before answering. "There is providence in every little thing, my friend. You should know I have been talking to your sister. You can scarcely have failed to note it, but she is a creature of rare and divine beauty, Henri."

"I trust it is so, but perhaps I see it with different eyes," I said. "But when were you talking to her? We have only been here two days, and she is a modest girl. You surprise me, Laertes."

"Not so much as I surprise myself," he said. "I was the happiest man alive but two hours ago. Now I am cast into a slough of despair."

I took him by the arm and enquired most earnestly what he might mean by this strange shift.

"This letter, it is indeed from Reynaldo. At least now I understand his skulking demeanour. He was bid by my father follow me to Paris, but not to introduce himself. Instead, he was to discover my habits, who my acquaintance were, what hours and company I kept at night - I told you, my father is not the most open of men. I congratulate myself that he could have heard no more than that I had struck up friendship with you, Lamor, which I believe is to my honour."

"Well, I hope it is not to your discredit, dear friend," I said. "But what is the matter of the letter? What does this Reynaldo have to say that distracts you so?"

"I am sorry, Lamor, I must indeed seem distracted. But what the letter says is enough to daze a man. A terrible tragedy has befallen me. Oh Henri, my father is killed! Dead at the hands of Prince Hamlet, by my word. The letter says that the prince is banished for his crime."

"What?" I cried. "Not punished further?"

"There is something to suggest that he performed the heinous act in an imperfect state of mind. I know not if that is what is being given out because he is the prince. It actually says here that there is doubt he knew who his victim was when he struck out at in his intemperate rage. But plainly I must return to Denmark on the instant."

I was struck quite dumb.

"There is the funeral to attend to, you see. But worse than that, my sister is made mad by the black devil's murderous act. She ever doted on him, for she was young in years. I need to be with her, Lamor."

I said I understood and engaged to take charge of all preparations and provisions for his journey myself. "You must leave us, I see, on the morrow," I said sadly. "But courage, man..."

"I know," he said. "But this is not all. This blow descends on one already struck by a dread bolt."

"You mean that your sister is torn between her loss and her feelings for the prince?" I said.

"Not even that. It is I, Lamor. Fair Eloise has robbed me of my heart. Now I must leave forthwith and bear the charge of your sister's heart on my travels, I fear."

"What say you?" I roared. "What nonsense is this? Why, man, you have but met her, had no more words with her than may cram up half a page of a maiden's journal! You measure this as loss to weigh against a kinsman's death! Why, not just kinsman, but your own fountainhead! Your father, by our Lord!"

"My father was a dolt. My sister is worth ten of him. But mark, Lamor, your sister is worth twenty of her, I trow."

I had my hand on my dagger hilt at this, but I managed to refrain.

News of death can shake a man to senselessness, I saw.

"Eloise is fair," I said, "And none of nobler birth lives in all of Normandy. But you mistake, Henri. She is but fifteen years of age, by God!"

"A tender heart untrammelled by the cage of years. But mine own heart is just as tender, I swear by Jove!"

"Swear by every Roman god and more," I rejoined. "You'll not traduce my sister, man! Or you will answer with your heart. Ay, and your liver too!"

"I pray you, ease your mind," Laertes urged me. "I mean no harm to her or to your family. I will return when matters at home are resolved. Despite our bitter grief I feel sure Ophelia will be restored when once she sees me. Then I will return and pay court to Eloise in every due regard and form. Do not you doubt, my word is bond in this?"

I had to sit down. All the sudden release of emotion had quite baffled my senses and my proportionate thought.

"I know not what to say," I sighed. "You say this Hamlet is banished?"

"Quite so"

"Then there is no danger in your going home? No retribution, no policy or intrigue?"

"The King has sent the black villain off to England. There may he rot. If he is indeed mad they will scarcely notice it there. Denmark will be purified by his dismissal. As soon as I set my family affairs to rights, I will hasten back. When I return, if Eloise's heart is chaste and honest as I trust more than even you yourself may hold a truth, good Lamor, I will pay suit as father of mine own name and fortune."

Well, a pretty state, I thought. We talked into the night, and in the end I almost believed it true my friend had won my sister's affections at a stroke. But nonetheless I was glad of my rest that afternoon, for I scarcely slept a wink all night.

Laertes left next morn without formal adieus, leaving me to explain to my father and to sweet Eloise how things had come to this amazing pass. My poor sister did not shed a word, though she poured out her grief like a waterspout once left alone. My father ahemmed and hummed, but he merely shrugged and walked off to attend to the affairs of his estate for Laertes was nought but a visitor in his house. Naturally I could not betray my sister's and my friend's new tryst to him, for it would have meant a severe retribution for Eloise and doubtless some harsh words to myself for introducing a viper into the family home.

The next two days passed slowly by. I could not leave Eloise in her delicate state but knew she could not talk of Laertes without a moistened eye. In the end I felt I would be even glad to return to my studies with Ducroix. At fine, my parting from Eloise was some unknown type of sweet sorrow.

"Do you believe Laertes will return?" she asked me.

"Beyond a doubt," I said.

My sister touched her rosary and sighed in half-belief, half-doubt.

"He is a man I trust withal," I said. "I have known him ... long enough to warrant that at least."

I saw she had a posy at her breast of faded, fingered bluebells.

***

I am waiting now at Mme Garnier's for news from that far off frozen land. Laertes has been gone three weeks, but surely will return. I have, as I said at first, but little sense of smell, but May is not far off, and Mme Garnier tells me that her azaleas and her tulips are in full bloom and roses soon will blossom and fill the air with all the Summer's sanguine scents. I had a letter from Eloise yesterday and in the folds of it she pressed some rosemary and rue, for remembrance of her loving brother, as I construe.

THE MASTER'S MISSING HEART

There'd be some as'd say he didn't have no heart in the first place. I were his housekeeper for over ten years and he never had much of a word for I, I can tell 'ee. But I'll admit it, he did have feelings, and where do they come from, if not the heart, eh? She broke his feelings, that woman, if not his heart, that's certain sure. Of course, the master never said nothing to I about it. But I'd see him in the room up above our heads now, his back to me as he sat at his old desk, facing out to the garden in the big house. Did you have a good gander at the garden here afore you came in? The hollyhocks is just grand, ain't they? And the blue and white Canterbury bells? So much colour in that small patch of garden. It's as it was in the old days, you know, though of course that were before my time. A touch tidier, I suppose, to say the truth. Point of fact it were that overgrown when he was here. He loved colour and life and he always insisted on letting the flowers run free and wild. Too wild, if you ask me.

'Mrs T,' he said to me moran once, 'Regard the profusion. Take in the very gations. Those pansies are small, but they're powerful beings, you know, Mrs T. The garden is alive, and it's alive with a hundred species, all pushing and shoving at each other like a football crowd. A football crowd of flowers, Mrs T, all wearing their own team's colours.' He'd talk like that to me, you know. But all the time he'd never even turn and face me. Rubbing his tash with his old fingers and looking all glittery-eyed out at that little garden. Sometimes I think he were just practising his paragraphs on me. On anyone who had the time and leisure to stand around and listen, I guess. Not that I had time, mind. This is only a tiddly little house, I know, but there was fires to keep up at Max Gate and where there's fires there's dust. And where there's dust there's me, dust's natural enemy. And of course there was the baking and cooking. Very fond of his nourishment, he were.

35

Now I've never read any of 'em meself, but they say there's never mention of anyone having a meal in any of his book writing, apart from someone taking a pull at a cider flask, or crunching into a nice bit of crusty bread, mebbe. Now that struck me as funny. Funny peculiar, I mean, because his mind was rarely off of food the whole time I served him. I sometimes wonder what them dairy girls and fine young gentlemen he wrote about got up to half the time, if they never sat down for a good hot dinner. But books are a bit of a mystery to me generally, I have to say. People making whole speeches to each other as if they was in parliament or something, heh heh. It's not life as folk live it, is it? Despite him setting himself up as the voice of Dorset, or whatever he thought he was. Though actually they tell I he never used the word - never so much as named the county. Someone in the Farmer's Arms was saying about it. Heared it on a radio programme. It was Jack Widdington, matter of fact, owns a lorry haulage firm outside Dorchester. Jack don't never read a book neither, not even an almanac, scarce more a reading book, but he heared a programme they broadcasted on Mr Hardy. They said it was a made-up county he wrote about, only it had all the same villages we got. I'm from Poole originally, which is nearly Hampshire, as you know, but I rather think I'd stick to the names places have had all these years, if I was going to sit down and tell stories, not go making up towns and so forth. If I was setting out to tell the real truth of Dorsetshire, I mean.

But I know what you're most interested in, don't I? That business about Westminster Abbey and the cat, I daresay. Well, I do happen to know the truth, and it's something of a story, I can tell 'ee. But it's none too comfortable on my old bones, this kitchen chair. What do you say about us retiring to a hostelry I know not too far from here? It'd take me a good half hour, mebbe, to tell the story properly, and we can have a proper sit-down there. Perhaps a drop of barley wine to ease the telling too, eh?

**

Now that's better, ain't it? I know it's only this old rexene, but it's snug enough here by a good fire and an arm to rest my elbow on. Well then,

I'll begin at the beginning, which is quite right, and what the master always said you had to do. Imagine the scene, if you will. Mid January, a mizzly afternoon. The oaks have long since stripped themselves for their winter bed, so to speak, but there's not been a frost all winter and there's still quite a leafy mulch on the ground. I mention it for good reason, you understand, not just to paint you an old watercolour of the countryside, like them tuppenny ha'penny pictures you get on the walls of coffee shops and the like. The leaves are all rotted away, but they're damp from a recent fall of rain, or perhaps the dew is still on 'em. They're just soft enough to take the impression of somebody's footprint and hold it for later inspection anyhow. Now you'll mark I said footprint, not paw print. Oh yes, there's an animal in the tale alright, but we're not concerned with all the little paw prints there may be round the garden. Though cats are light enough on their paws, ain't they? Perhaps there ain't no paw prints. Anyway, I stray from my tale. Hey, did you hear that? Stray! Tail! But this is a serious story, not one of a humorous bent, so don't let me starting chuckling now, will 'ee?

The point is, there's footprints on the path up to the back door of the cottage. And they weren't made by the men from the funeral director's, no. The men came in through the front door, as is right. Nobody as should have been in the house that day went out the back, see? Nobody except me, I mean, and the marks on the soggy leaves weren't the marks of a size three court shoe, I can tell 'ee. I had them shoes new on that fateful day. Black, of course, which don't normally suit me, but they were a nice shoe. Expensive. My feet have swoll since, so I couldn't wear 'em now, even if I chose to, but I still got 'em up in my loft somewhere. Sentimental, I suppose, though some'd say not so much as folk would normally notice.

But I ought to carry on with trying to set you the scene, didn't I? As I say, it was a muggy, drizzly old day and we all had overcoats on. It kind of made the room look smaller, us standing there like dray shires, steaming and blowing out cold air through our nose holes. There's Dr Mann, a gaunt looking old bird with bony long fingers - much like as if they was a bird's talons in truth - and he's talking to the gentleman they've got down from over Bournemouth way for the operation. Well, I say operation, it's more of a dissection, to be honest. He's a specialist, you see, but he don't look like one. He hasn't got a white coat on or nothing. He takes his astrakhan greatcoat off and just puts on a green rubber apron. He's got a little black suitcase with scalpels and such all neatly lined up when he opens the lid, like a larger sort of pencil case, actually. So he takes a scalpel and stands there, not saying a word. Of course, the master was still all buttoned up in his suit and tie and we all looked at each other as if to say, 'Who's going to undo his shirt then, boys?' But Nellie Titterinton - she was the new maid after I was dismissed, but that's not a story I care to go into right now - Nellie darts forward and starts trying to open the shirt front. The trouble is, the shirt is fresh starched and it's as stiff as a piece of three ply, and Nellie's struggling with the buttons as if they was fake ones, or like she was trying to open a jar of jam with butter greased fingers. It's getting just a touch embarrassing for all concerned, you might say. So old talon fingers leans forward.

'Let me do that, Mrs Trapp,' says he. Nellie looks disappointed, but she knows her place, Dr Mann being a figure of respect in Dorchester for several years at that time. She might have blushed, but you'd never be able to tell with Nellie 'cause she had a complexion redder than a Victoria plum, rain or shine. The doctor can't get the damn things undone neither though, but he don't go red, he stays whiter than a page of writing paper. He just gives a bit of a cough. So the specialist gentleman - I don't rightly recall his name, but he was a something-something, you know, one of them double barrelled types - is starting to get hoity toity by this time. He says, 'Allow me, Dr Mann,' or something like that, you know the way they talk down in the city, and cool as a cucumber he steps forward and cuts off one of the buttons with his scalpel. I swear, it was like something out of Baroness Orczy - one quick swoosh, and the button slices off neat as a carrot top. Then he does the same with the next three buttons, and before you know it there's the master's pale white chest exposed to the light one last time.

Now you might expect what I'm going to tell you next to be real gory and stomach churning, but it ain't. I was expecting the blood to come spurting out when that scalpel went into his poor chest, but no such thing. All we got was a sticky black ooze, like as if it was molasses, not blood that was in there. I didn't get to see the bone-breaking part because I was ushered out of the chamber at that moment by Dr Mann. He said it weren't right for females to witness what had to be done next, so me and Nellie had to wait outside. But I heared it all right from the dressing room next door. Snap, snap, snap, like the remains was no more than chicken bones. The consultant had a kind of pliers, he did, to lever apart the ribs and get at the poor man's entrails. I'd been asked to put the kettle on, so I couldn't hear anything that was said, if indeed they did do any talking, against the sound of the steam whistling away. Me and Nellie looked at each other all solemn. Then we had to get on with the business of brewing up for the doctors.

You'll mebbe have heard the next part, where the heart gets put on a marble slab that was on the trestle table. Well, it weren't so. And that's how I know no cat come and jumped up and took it away into the bushes to feed off of. For one thing the back door was closed all the time. It were a cold January day, as I said. For another, the doctor laid out the organ on a special muslin cloth he had. Laid it out, then wrapped it up in a bundle, as if it were no more than a dollop of curds. Then he put it in a wooden container he'd brought along for the purpose. It were like a miniature coffin, except of course there weren't no brass handles etcetera. It had a proper hinged lid. Now, you never see a cat opening a box with a lid, have you? Also, I had my eye on that box the whole time I was in there, while the two doctors did what they had to do in making good the corpse. By which I mean the clearing up and the pinning back of Mr Hardy's shirt front and so forth. Adams - he were the funeral director - then gets his men to lift the body into the waiting coffin and he screws down the lid himself. Oh, funny thing, I just remembered the specialist gentleman's name - it were How White. Idn't that remarkable? Dr How White, it's not like a proper name, is it? But I recall it now, and I swear that's what he were called.

Anyway, I've thought about what happened next over and over. The carriage was outside, and Adams and his men must have gone out to open up the doors, I suppose. Dr Mann and Dr White went into the kitchen to wash their hands and such like. I know I'd gone round the side of the house to throw the old tea leaves from the pot into the bin. That leaves Nellie Titterinton, who could have been left alone in the parlour with the master and the little wooden box for a few minutes, but I've spoke to her numerous times and she swears blind she was in the kitchen taking down some seedcake for Dr Mann. He was very partial to the flavour of caraway, I can vouch for that meself. So if it wasn't Nellie who took the heart, it had to be an intruder. Which brings us back to the footprints in the back garden. I don't know why, but as it happened I chose not to go back into the house the way I'd come out. I walked round the side and up to the back door. That's when I saw the footprints on the leaf mulch. Deep ridged marks they were, like off a gumboot. Now I know I said they weren't delicate little footprints from a size three court shoe, but they weren't a man's prints neither. If I were a Scotland Yard detective or something, I'd have to say they was made by somebody wearing a lady's wellington boot. There, I've given the game away, haven't I?

Well, perhaps I haven't after all. I can tell by your expression you're misdoubting me now. But everything I say is the gospel truth. If Nellie were here now she'd confirm it, whatever else she'd be like to say about me. Unfortunately, I didn't have the presence of mind to say nothing about there being these footprints in the back garden when I went back in the house. My mind was on other things, naturally. I sort of took them in unconscious like, and it was only later when they come to have the service at Stinsford that I realised what must have took place. I mean, nobody said anything, but it was the expression on the pastor's face as he took the box to place it in the earth next to poor Mrs Emma's grave. Like as if he knew it were too light to contain a human heart, though of course some says that they put half a pound of calf's liver in there instead, to make up the weight, so to speak. There were a look of concern on the reverend's features that suggested to me anyway that he had a feeling that what he were doing were a blasphemy. Mayhap he felt he were doing something unusual in burying a part of a man who'd already been burned and was having his ashes buried elsewhere, up in the abbey. It could have been just that, but I didn't think so, not from his face. And of course, the rumours had already started. About the moggy escaping with what she regarded as a bit of four day old offal, I mean. Nobody could say whose cat it were though, which I find rather suspicious. This is how things go, ain't it? Someone says, 'I bet it were the cat stole his heart,' and then everyone's telling you precisely the order of events, except for key details, like the name of the blessed animal.

It was Mrs Hardy - the second one, I mean, Miss Dugdale as was - that was to blame for most of it. She brung out her book about him the same year. That's abnormally fast writing, you may well say, even if the second half didn't come out till two years later. And after the master said he didn't want people to go into all that stuff. She covered up whatever she liked, or whatever she didn't like, I should say, and folk started doubting what they knew for certain facts. I'll tell you certain sure facts though. Fact (a) is he were a proper mean man. That's a documentary fact. I'm sorry to have to say it, but the truth needs to be heared from time to time, dunnit? Fact (b) is he never forgot about Miss Tryphena. I know, I know, they was family anyway, but there's more to it than that, let me tell you. A lot more. Fact (c) is that blessed wire haired terrier of his, but I won't go into that. It weren't the dog, just like it weren't no cat. The truth is, and I've come to it now, the master lost his heart years before it disappeared out of that funny little hinged box. And I don't mean he lost it to a woman neither. That's what they say, ain't it? "He lost his heart to her!" But what I'm saying is, he let it go missing, just as good as if it had been took out by that vicious shiny little scalpel fifty years afore. By which I don't mean to say he mislaid it with Mistress Emma, mind. Nor even with that slip of a schoolteacher, Miss Sparks. What I mean to say is, he put it into his books. Laid it between the pages like a young girl pressing a fresh picked flower. And when you open a book of his, they say, there it is, a poor dried up thing, but still in its proper shape. Well, I can see you think I'm being a trifle fanciful now, but it's true.

Let me tell you a secret. Hey, one more of these barley wines and I'll be telling the world about its mother, won't I? But serious, I'll tell you something about Mrs Florence So-Called Hardy. She never wrote those books on him. She might have wrote the words down, I grant, but they weren't her words, do you see? It was the master what wrote the whole of it, as if those two volumes were just two more of his reading books. Now you'd think at the age of eighty-some he'd think to let a bit of his true heart out, wouldn't you? But it ain't so. He didn't want a biography as such. He wanted another novel, that's what, with himself as the character at the heart of things. He gave her all the papers, all the letters and whatnot, and he dictated the bits betwixt and between. And he never mentioned a word of yours truly. Can you imagine that? Ten years! A decade of serving and slaving and at the end of it all I don't exist, except as you see me now, a woman of advanced years, it has to be said, and truly, not in the best of health. Though this little drink has helped a bit, I'll say that. But folk don't have the time of day for me, not even here in Higher Bockhampton. But you ask after me in Dorchester or Weymouth or up in Blandford and they'll look at you blank. Nellie Titterington, oh yes, they'll tell you she were a fine woman. A hard worker and a faithful employee. Them gentlemen from Lunnon as come down and took photographs of the old house and traced back all the lines and lineages. Them critics and historians. They talked to Mistress Florence; they spent hours over their port and sherry and fancy Havana cigars talking to Miss Eva and all the famous friends who liked to call in at Max Gate after my time. But they never had a word for me, no. I'm a pariah of this parish, I'll tell 'ee, and that's the sad truth of it. I will partake of one of those cheroots of yours, if you don't mind offering me one. Helps the breathing, they say. Thank you kindly. Now what was I saying?

Oh, the heart of the matter, as you might say. Yes, it did go missing. Some say as one of Adams' men went sneaking back into the house and took it back to his missus. Others swear the cat got his heart, though it never got his tongue, I have to say that, waggle it as the master did all his life. So many words. They say he wrote upwards of two dozen reading books. And more poems than you could shake a good ashplant at. But all them writings was from another organ than as has ventricles and articles - arteries, whatever you call 'em. Jack Widdington read me one of them poems once. Laughed, he did, after he done the reading out too. Said, "That's you, Mrs Trapp, to a T. The interloper." It weren't true. I never loped into anything that wasn't my business. I'm sure the master couldn't have wrote that stuff about me. "I wish she weren't here," or some such.

That's Emma Gifford, that is. I told old Jack. Or Miss Sparks. It ain't me, I tell you.

Oh look! Out there. A sun shower. Rain and sun at the same time. Now ain't that a strange thing? It marks me of the time the master spoke to me about his early days here in Bockhampton. It were the same weather that day, bright as a button but rain falling like angels' tears on the summer grass. He weren't exactly telling me as a person, you know, but he was saying it out loud, and he must have known I were in the room dusting. I think that's how he chose to talk to me, as if I was a ghost like, but knowing I were real enough, in his heart of hearts. Or perhaps I should say in his mind of minds, eh? Anyway, he starts his reminiscing, then he says something strange.

"The art is in the concealment of the art," he says. By which I took him to really be talking about his heart, even though I didn't hear no aitch in the word. I says, "That's true, Mr H." I were thinking about my cleaning, to tell the truth, and I was referring to that great art of the housemaid - to make things look clean by sweeping the dust under the coverings, if you get my meaning. I'll tell you something else now I'm retired from the housekeeping trade, you can place a goodly dab of polish out of sight in a room so as it catches a draught and makes the whole room smell fresh as Spring. Save yourself a whole deal of trouble that way. I don't know if the master was wise to that old trick, but I do know we was understanding each other well enough that time when he spoke of concealment as he did. Even if we wasn't really talking about the same thing on the surface level of things. But I felt sorry for him that time, him thinking about his childhood and remembering his old mother and all.

It's my theory, to tell you the truth, that nobody's whole. Not me, not the master, and certainly not Florence Hardy. Why, you're looking at me as if I'm starting to go on a ramble, but I'll explain my meaning. It's as if we's all born as half of ourselves, and our mission in life is to find the other half. Now, a lot of folk talk about their husband or wife as if they're the other half, but I don't mean that exactly. The missing part may be another person, though, mind, if you'd met my old man Trapp

43

you'd probably doubt he'd even make up a half. But the missing part may be something else. A job, say. Or a religion, if you're that way inclined. Mebbe even a friend, like the master had Mr Moule as his friend. Least, until the poor man took his own life. They say Lord Tennyson had a friend that he lost to the waves, don't they? And he was never a whole man again after the tragedy, I believe. Now I lost a child that was the other half of me. More, perhaps. So I've never been whole since. But I could have got back to some sort of roundness if I hadn't been wrote out of the story, I feel. But there it is, I don't feel no bitterness about it.

But the master, his half that he was always a-looking for was right there inside him all the time. But he couldn't see the wood for the trees, despite his fondness for our Dorset country, as you may say. It's one of those strange coincidences, ain't it? Him being a stonemason and then him letting his heart turn to stone like that. It's like he spent all those long years whittling away at himself to make a fancy carving of the man he wanted to be, when all he had to do was feel the pumping inside and recognise that there weren't nothing missing after all. That he had his heart in-tacked and he was a whole man. But he'd boxed it up, so to say. There's the business of Miss Tryphena, of course, and that explains a fair deal of it. She were his cousin alright, but they was closer than first cousins, and that's the truth of it. He could never have married her, is all I'm saying. And they hushed up the child. A lot of it goes on still, to this day. I won't say no more about that, but I could if I wanted to. But, the times being the times, what does a man like the master do? He digs deep inside and tears out the part that's given him so much grieving, that's what he does. Then he tells story after story about people making the very same sort of mistake and destroying themselves and their families, as if that's going to act as a warning to others. I tell 'ee, it takes a cold hearted villain to do that, when all's said and done. I told him myself.

"Listen, Mr H," I says. "You can't get away from it, you loved Miss Tryphena and she loved you. She'll be bearing a sign of that love, and you recognising that sign is what is going to make you a whole man." He never listened. He stared out of the window and didn't say nothing but that the pansies was in their prime and the apple blossom was whiter than a funeral shroud, whatever that was supposed to mean. He had an old piano that was always in full gleam from the polishing it had. I was looking at it as I spoke to him and I saw his refection in it, sort of blurry, but clear enough nonetheless. He'd half turned round, which was something he never normally did in my presence, I don't know if I said that already, but that was when I saw that his heart was gone forever. He looked at me as if I was the sphinx and he said: "Mrs Trapp, I believe there are some things best left unsaid." Now, that was from a man who tried all his life to say things that the gentry insisted shouldn't be spoke about. I picked up my polish and my cloth and made ready to leave, for I couldn't respond to a harsh rebuke like that, but he spoke again. "The serving classes are not usually in a position to see these things, I know, but it's something you would do well to bear in mind."

I ask you! He were from the craftsman classes, I know, though his mother were from ordinary stock and as poor as a church mouse, and she did well in catching the elder Mr Hardy. But what a thing to say to a woman who'd given him ten years of her life! Well, I have borne it in mind these long years. And it's only now I choose to speak. I realise at last I would like to make my mark, so to speak. And that's what I'm relying on, talking to you like this.

No, I won't have another glass, warming though it is. We're getting certain looks from those gentlemen by the bar, and it may well be time for me to go back to my cottage. The rain is coming on harder, look at it ploughing down that pane. I must leave you. I won't pester you with my hurts any more. You can tell your readers what you choose to. You can stick to that old cat story if you like. Or say that it's all nonsense, and the master's heart is safe in the ground beneath Stinsford cemetery, though it beats on in the heart of the country - I know how you writers like to make things sound grand. But I'd pray you at least mention me, tell them my part in things. Say I was a simple country woman, and that I talked too much and said too little, if that's your way, but don't deny me my part.

What's that? Oh, I never said, did I? It's Edie I've always been known as, though my real name's Frieda. I was named for the day I was

45

born, you see. And that old rhyme is right enough too. I always did work hard for a living, I can tell 'ee, though there'll never be any mark of it left after I've gone. Not so much as that lady's print in the mulched up leaves. I spent a lifetime cleaning up round the edges of great men, wiping up their dust, which they tell me is mainly made of the little flakings of their skin, though I don't like to think of it like that. But the dust has a habit of descending faster than you can dispel it, doesn't it?

Mmm? Oh, no, I never said, did I? I think it were the work of an insider, not an interloper. But there, I've told you how I'd like it set down. I don't doubt you'll say what you want to say, or write it like your readers'll want to read it, I suppose. Biographies is just versions of things, ain't they? If I were to write out my own times it's only be a version of the truth. Parts missing, parts not as others would recall 'em. You never know, mebbe if I can find the words I'll do it too, one day.

SIMON'S NAVEL

"Omphalos!" cried the ragged man on the peak. His wild mop of shaggy hair had once been a rich black, but it was now speckled grey through wear, care and age, though it gave the appearance of being lightly dusted with chalk or ash rather than growing grey from the roots as the result of pigmentation loss. He was naked to the waist, except for a narrow leather band tied round his wrist as a crude bracelet. His lower limbs were partly covered by a dirty brown loin cloth, or foreshortened kilt, and his feet were unshod, though there were remnants of a dull blue paint or varnish on his stubby toenails. Round his feet, as he sat cross-legged, arms hugging each other on his narrow rock plateau, were the unsavoury scraps of that morning's, and possibly the previous day's, meal. In his big deep brown eyes and in his torpid demeanour there was somehow less of a man and more of a thinner, browner gorilla, it occurred to me. He seemed to be waiting for me to speak.

"Hail, master," I said.

"In my beginning is my end," he said. His voice was cracked and reedy, but still quite resonant in the rarer air of the plateau.

"May I call you by your given name, master?" I said. "Mine is Roger. Roger Penman."

"You may call me Simeon, or Simon if you prefer," he said. "Here there are no names of trades or places - only that which is touched by holy water and the hand of the minister." He looked down at his lap in apparent modesty as I crouched down awkwardly, trying to put myself at his level for further talk. I was aware that there was something of the supplicant in my posture, my hands resting on one knee and my trailing leg bent back behind me. My limbs were already threatening to ache anyway, so I adjusted my position and attempted to ape his yogic squat. When I was comfortable enough I spoke again:

"Hail, Simon. I believe it is an anniversary of sorts for you?"

He nodded almost imperceptibly. "Thirty nine years on this pillar of rock," he said. "It is a long time."

"Well," I said, "It certainly is that. You are nothing if not a patient man, may I say."

"I am both," he replied, this time with a flash of a twisted incisor that reminded me more of a bear than a gorilla. I guess though that it was the first muscle spasm of a sardonic smile.

"I beg your pardon?"

"I am, as you say, a patient man. I am also nothing, or as nothing."

"Well, I wouldn't say that exactly ..."

"But you did. And I do. You see, we are getting on famously already. The secret of communication is agreement, is it not?"

I started to say I wasn't so sure about that, but I saw the thin brown upper lip curling back again and an incisor preparing to unsheath itself once more. I understood he had been attempting some form of humorous remark. Thirty nine years on a mountain top does little to refine a man's comic sensibilities, however, and my mission was too urgent to incline me to laughter. I wiped a bead of perspiration from my underlid, where it had meandered down from my brow.

"I thought it would be colder," I said. I am not a man to miss an opportunity of phatic talk, and it seemed like a good idea to recommence our dialogue on a fairly neutral topic.

"Is it warmer in the valley then?" he said. He sounded genuinely surprised at my observation and I sensed a danger that we were about to embark on rather too exhaustive an exchange about meteorological matters. I quickly pointed out that it had been an arduous climb. Forty feet, measured vertically, was climatically insignificant, I would have liked to say, but I feared it might sound like a rebuke.

"Anyway, I think not of valleys and mountains," he said. "They are not the mind, but the body of the earth. The breasts and the belly and the groin you might say. They are but an impasto sweep of God's hand over the creation."

"Indeed," I said. I was trying to find my pencil and notebook, which I had somewhere in my pouch but could not for the moment locate. "I imagine the mind is taken with more metaphysical issues at this remove. Over a period of thirty nine years, at least."

"As you say. The bear does not count the trees, and neither does the porpoise the waves. Why should I think of the land any more than I do the sky? They are above and below ..."

"The other way round, I think you'll find," I tried to interject, but I think my utterance went unheard. Perhaps it was just as well.

"And what is here, and what is now, and what will always be, is the space between. I mean the black hole that is the only connection."

"Connection?"

"Between life and death, birth and dissolution, the womb and the tomb."

I'd found my pencil and notebook by now. I wrote down the last phrase, though more out of a desire to start writing than for the felicity of the phrase, or indeed for its meaningfulness to me.

"So ..."

"Yes?"

"Thirty nine years, eh?"

He picked up a piece of discarded melon and inspected the rind with a thumbnail. "A lifetime for some men." He threw down the mouldy segment. "No little time for me, as a matter of fact. But I would do it again."

"Really?" I scrutinised the big brown eyes, which were pointed at me, but fixed on some horizon way beyond me, I suspected.

"Well, I do not suppose the lord will grant me so much time again. I am already of an age when a man looks to his past rather than his future

49

to make sense of his presence. I think I will rest here one more year, however."

"But you already hold the record," I started to say. "By several months, I believe. Is there any point in carrying on?"

"Is there any point in starting? But we do, and then there are only two options - keep on keeping on, or give up."

"That's a very stoical attitude," I said.

"Indeed."

There was something of a lull at this point, and it almost seemed as if he had forgotten about my presence. "Would you say you had achieved anything by your sojourn?" I asked. He turned his head away and gazed at the blue hills in the distance.

"Apart from the record, you want to say?"

"Well, yes, apart from the record, of course. Not that I want to belittle that achievement, naturally. It's not likely to be beaten, is it?"

"Not in my lifetime," he laughed. "Unless you know something to the contrary. Is there a younger man somewhere in Ephesus perhaps, on a taller tower, with better provisions? A man with more loyal friends perhaps, and with a stronger sense of his own destiny? I find it hard to imagine if there be such a man, and that he may be more dedicated to his god, but who can tell?"

I told him I knew of no such pretender, though it was possible that his own example might prompt others to follow in course of time. I doubted whether anyone would display his tenacity and patience, however, and I told him that too.

"Let it be as it is," he said.

I asked him if he would mind answering a few personal questions. He shook his head gently, and to my mind with some sadness. I quickly began on my prepared list, for fear he would drift off into the trance that his torpor continually threatened.

"Firstly," I said, "Why this peak? It is a fair way up, I admit, but as you see, a man of little vitality like myself can reach it with only a modest enough effort."

"The mountain is inside the man," he said.

"Okay, well, might I ask what plans you had in the first place to ... well, frankly, to pass the time?"

"Time will pass without our planning," he answered in a dry, level voice. "Its passage only needs marking if you fear it is being wasted."

"That's probably very true," I urged, "But there must have been moments, - hours perhaps, days even - when you were tearing your hair out with the boredom ..."

"Boredom is another word for fear of your own insignificance. That is not something I fear, though it is something of which I am certain."

"So I suppose you've found plenty of things to think about, over the years?" It was a fairly desperate question, I knew, but I needed to get him off his cryptic, and somehow rehearsed, responses.

"I have thought," he replied slowly, "And I have banished thought. I have looked. I have listened. I have smelled the air and tasted the frost in winter, the oleanthus, the cypress and the olive in summer. I have been a man and done what men may do."

"Mmm," I said. "Though not perhaps as fully as some men. Which brings me to another question. Have you not missed the company of, well, your fellow men, for instance?"

His eyes focused on mine for the first time since I'd crouched down. "By that I think you perhaps mean the company of a woman. Is that not true?"

"Well, that too," I said. "The thought unavoidably crosses one's mind."

"It crosses or it does not cross. According to taste. Thoughts are not arrows, they are birds. They wing where they will."

I rather felt the need for a woman was more like an arrow than a sparrow myself, so his response gave me some pause. I had to suddenly consider the possibility that I was barking up the wrong mountain and I wondered whether I should rephrase the question to include the possibility of same sex company. I preferred to proceed down the avenue I had begun on, however, rather than turn down one of those darker side streets. "Perhaps we should just say fellow men as in fellow human beings," I ventured.

He smiled his pointy smile. "You are a young man," he said. "Though not as fit as a young man should be." I'd just wiped another errant droplet of sweat from the bridge of my nose and I was forced to shrug that it might be so. "But," he continued, "As a man who has many years before him, you are entitled to ask such things of an older man. I have thought, I say again, and I have banished thought."

"So, it's been difficult, eh?" I said, trying not to sound too animated.

"A man may travel a million miles by staying still," he said. "And a man may come to the greatest truth by refusing to pursue smaller truths."

This was dangerously cryptic again, and scarcely very quotable stuff. I pressed him. "How conscious were you that you were giving up normal human relations, would you say, when you chose to ascend to this peak?"

"I made a covenant with my eyes," he said, a sly look crossing his gnarled features, "Why then should I think upon a maid?"

"Well," I said, "I guess you also had to make a covenant, as you call it, with your ears. To give up the sounds of human discourse, I mean. That must be an even bigger loss in some ways. I know some monks take a vow of silence, but they've still got each other at least, haven't they, in some sense? Walking around, seeing other people making the commitment, sort of thing ... you're on your own completely up here ..."

He was listening patiently but I could tell he wanted to speak, and I trailed off at this point.

52

"When the ear heard me," he said slowly, and I sensed he was running a tape in his head again, "Then it blessed me. But men groan from out of the city, and I'm spared all that moaning ... all those execrations, at the end of the day."

I wanted to write: 'Barking mad' in my notebook, but it had been a long climb up sharp flinty rocks, and I had a deadline. I needed copy. But then before I could frame my next question he started speaking again. And it was pure gold.

"Of course, there was a girl once," he said. "I suppose there always is. But this girl ... oh, let me tell you. Her name was Esther, and she had eyes of honey, flesh of milk, a touch like the feather light touch of a mayfly on your arm, of a day old lamb against your side, of the petals of the rain on your cheek in May. And her thighs ... well, perhaps it is better not to speak of those ..."

"Age?" I said. "And, if you don't mind, hair colour?" I had a feeling 'petals of the rain' would be viewed as a misprint or something. You have to build a picture in ways the reader expects you to.

"She had hair of amber." His voice was as petally as inclement weather in early summer now and I had to lean forward to catch each word. "It flowed like a mountain spring. It tumbled and sashayed down over her shoulders like wine being poured. I think she was fifteen, but naturally she told me she was older than that ..."

I was writing feverishly: 'Strawberry blonde Esther (15) claimed she was innocent, and had been subjected to several months of harassment at the hands of this man ...' He stopped speaking as he saw that I was putting down so much.

"But you don't have to mention that," he said. "Though you could keep the bit about her hair flowing like wine poured. Perhaps you could use a bit of licence and say mead. That would be better still."

"Mead," I echoed. "And, I'm sorry to pry, but ... er ... general shape? Lissom, maybe? Or buxom. Voluptuous, if you prefer."

"Her form was as the early colt - gamine but yet fully shaped, if you get my drift. Who can say if the snowdrop or the lily be formed more perfectly? They are as they are - full flower, white as each other but white as only themselves. I do not speak of their form, for that would be murder to dissect. Wouldn't you agree?"

"I'm not all that big on flowers," I confessed. "She was a pretty little thing, and maybe destined to be a bit taller, but still of course pretty as ever - that's all I'm getting here."

"It is enough," he sighed.

"So what happened then, exactly, then?"

He gave me a Giaconda smile, only slightly more wrinkly. "It was not to be," he said. "I was not a whole man, you see."

I looked up from my notebook. "Really?"

His eyes started to glaze over and I was afraid I might not get to the important bit. "In what way, if you don't mind me asking? I mean ..."

There was a wry smile on his face again. "It is understandable that you are thinking what you are thinking," he said softly. "You are a young man, and as such you probably cannot prevent your thoughts constantly returning to one matter. No, I do not mean I am a eunuch, though of course I might as well be, given my choice of life these last four decades. But in a strange way it was worse than that, though perhaps you cannot imagine anything worse."

I tried to nod and shake my head at the same time. It must have looked like I had a flea in my ear that I was trying to dislodge. "It's not important what I may think," I managed to say. "But I am intrigued. In what way did you think of yourself as incomplete, I wonder?"

"I am surprised you have not seen for yourself," he said.

This of course made me want to scrutinise him more closely, for I certainly hadn't noticed anything. There was nothing as glaring as, say, a missing limb. It had to be something less obvious, like a glass eye, a missing sense of smell, or a missing finger or two. At the same time my sense of courtesy, or humility, was telling me not to stare, but to keep my

54

gaze at a normal level, and just carry on looking back at his face.

"I really couldn't guess," I said. "It's nothing very apparent anyway."

"Perhaps not," Simon said. "But a lover is inclined to examine the parts of his partner, or her partner in this case, slightly more assiduously."

"Well that's true," I said, thinking about my happy tryst with a servant girl called Ruth a few nights before. There is no denying that you can't help picking up the odd mole or little white hyphen scar, even when you're ostensibly just luxuriating in your nakedness next to a warm, willing night-mate. And to me there's a fair deal of pleasure in the noting, I might add. Plainly though, for Simon, it was different from one of those little defects or blemishes which can actually make a person more attractive. There was something absent from his person rather than something about his person that had turned this Esther girl right off.

"You see," he said, "I have no navel."

I couldn't help instantly lowering my eyes to his midriff. It was true. I was astonished that I hadn't noticed its absence. He was, as I think I've mentioned before, a lean, sinewy man, but there was still a narrow belt of folded-over flesh as he leaned forward, his elbows on his knees. Maybe it was this tight roll which had disguised the missing mark of humanity. But now I saw indeed that there was no indentation, no protuberant little concha of flesh, no slit, no cavity, no dark hole where an umbilicus had shrunk and shrivelled and retired into itself.

"Well, that's amazing," I said. "But how can it be? You are, I take it, born of woman, surely?"

"I never knew my mother," he said, "But I am not an alien from another planet. I suckled at a woman's breast. I came, wilful, wet and wriggling, from a woman's womb. I grew from a sullen seed to a perfect - well, not quite perfect, as I say, - but a pretty decent replica of a miniature human being. All in the normal nine months of gestation. My father assured me it was so."

I was writing feverishly. This was better than the underage sex story.

Navel-less Man Found on Syrian Mountain was already bannering itself up in 24 point across my subber's style sheet. "But you never knew your mum, you say? Never got a chance to talk to her about your, well, I don't know how to put it, your pristine expanse of buttonless tummy?"

"She died in the act of giving me life."

"Oh, I'm sorry about that," I said quickly. "Is your father still alive, by any chance?" I could really have done with a quote on this one.

"My father would be ninety three if God had chosen to let him continue in this coil. No, he is gone before too."

"Mmm. Sorry to hear that."

"But you must be wondering how I was sustained in the womb," he said.

I put down my quill. "Yes, that's a bit of a puzzler," I said. "But you don't know the answer to that, do you? How could you?"

"Obviously I do know not know empirically, or should I say, by act of memory. But I have spent some time in consideration of this riddle, I can assure you."

It occurred to me that a man could spend quite a while on such an enigma. Still, thirty nine years was maybe pushing it. "You mean that is what prompted you to abnegate society? Or abdicate it. You know what I'm trying to say ..."

"I think I knew before you even started to say it, Roger. Not talking to another human soul means you tend to commune rather a lot with your own, you know. The result is that you somehow know more about other people than if you were constantly around them, I find. I hope you don't find that too presumptuous?"

"No, of course not," I said. "Feel free. Well, I suppose you already do, in some sense."

"Indeed."

"So," I said, "Without empirical evidence, what's your theory?"

He looked up at a camel-shaped cloud that was passing low overhead. I followed his gaze and watched as a gust of wind made the cumulo-soft strands reshape themselves into a different sort of hump-backed creature.

"My theory?" Simon said, returning to earth, so to speak. "I think there is destiny in all things. What God makes whole, he intends to be consummate and at one with itself. What God sunders, he sunders for a reason. The lightning-struck sycamore and the harelip child are but the signs of the Almighty's sword."

I nodded. "I was thinking more about your theory regarding your missing navel," I said. "Although you must excuse me if I missed the point in what you just said."

"Ah yes. Well, it's true that I have a theory about that specifically too."

"Un hunh. And ...?"

"But first you must tell me why you think man is marked in this way. Shot through the middle by the bolt of birth, if you will allow me a piece of figurative language."

"Ah yes, good. Bolt, mmm. Though I suppose that would apply more to innies than outies, wouldn't it?"

"Excuse me?"

I realised that the delightful configurations of the whorl of an indented belly button, and the strange worm cast of flesh of a convex arrangement, were inevitably a mystery to this man. Though surely he must have seen Esther (15)'s bare abdomen. mustn't he?

"Um, some people have like a bullet hole," I said. "Others have a fleshy sticky-outy bit. It's all to do with the length of cord that the midwife leaves, I think. Actually, I've never thought about the causes for the difference. Mine's an inny, which is sort of neater, but does attract an unfortunate deposit of lint or wool, depending on whether I wear calico or sheepskin. Or where I sleep, perhaps it is."

"You make it sound like the pouch of an animal, or a Scotsman's sporran."

I wondered how he knew about kangaroos, or wallabies. Or Scottish tribal costume, come to that. He was certainly more *au fait* with the wide world than a man might reasonably be expected to be, considering he hadn't left his pillar for nearly forty years. I decided to let that matter rest, however.

"Yes," I said, "You're right. A sort of pouch. Except smaller, naturally. And less use, if truth be told. It's not like enough lint or wool gathers for you to do anything with it, I mean. Unless you saved it up religiously, I suppose. I never thought to do that. I pick it out every month or so, when I take a bath. It can be quite a tricky manoeuvre actually. You don't want to use a sharp implement, you see. I use my little finger. Even then I sometimes stab myself with my nail."

Simon said that this was fascinating.

"Yes, well, we don't need to talk about that," I said. "But we do perhaps need to explore the mystery of how you were nourished during your nine months in the womb."

"I'd prefer to discuss the mystery of how men and women are made to bear this mark of their origins, or indeed perhaps their mortality ..."

"You reckon it's that?" I said, in some surprise.

"It's a stigma, is it not? Consider: your nostrils are tunnels for the passage of air; your ears caves where sounds may enter and reverberate; your mouth a spring for words or kisses and a harbour for food and drink. I could extend this description to account for other orifices too, but you follow my train of thought, I imagine."

"You mean, every hole has its function - to take in or expel?"

"Precisely so. If you count up you'll find it's seven orifices."

I did a quick calculation. Strictly, I thought, it's seven for a woman, minus the navel of course. Actually, eight for a man, if you chose to closely investigate the anatomy of the penis, with its double barrelled exit for urine and spermatozoa. It seemed churlish to correct Simon on this point.

"A magic number, you will agree?"

I nodded/shrugged.

"So why make it eight? Eight is symmetrical, and the number of infinity, I will grant you, but here we are not dealing with symmetry, are we? That would mean pairing up the navel with the mouth, wouldn't it? All the others work in some sort of tandem. But I can't see any connections between the instrument of speech and love and an inny or an outy, as you put it."

"A tree may have seven roots or eight roots," I said. "Symmetry doesn't come into it, it's just how the tree grows."

"I see you are enjoying our little dialectic," Simon said. This time he permitted himself a rasping sort of chuckle.

I apologised for my flowery (arboreal, in truth) analogy and told him I'd let him do the stuff about trees from then on. I'd content myself with making notes, and giving the conversation the occasional nudge in the direction of newsworthiness, if I could.

Actually, I'd embarked on this mission to get a story about a man who'd ostracised himself from his fellow man for half a lifetime. I'd had a working headline - *HERMIT TELLS ALL* - but that had dived off briefly into a different story - *JILTED LOVER TELLS OF HIS 39 YEAR LONELINESS* - but now it was altogether a more specialised piece that was taking on an interesting biological slant - *MAN WITH NO NAVEL TELLS ALL*. As soon as I'd abandoned my analogy about tree roots I tried to come up with a catchier headline. I flirted with HOLE-LESS HOLY MAN CLAIMS HOLINESS, but it was too pun-packed, even for my paper.

"A man may heal with prayer as well as medicine," he said, after a short lull. "But I discovered my difference before I committed myself to God in the way that you see me now."

"When was that then?" I asked. "When you were a child perhaps?

59

In the bath? Sports Day, when you were changing with the other chaps?"

"I do not remember the occasion, more the sense of separateness. That feeling has been with me a long time."

"Yes well, it would have," I said. "But if we could pin down when your navel disappeared, rather than posit that you never had one, we're over the problem of how you managed to grow when you were a foetus, aren't we? Say, if it sort of just grew over when you were toddling about, we're dealing with more of a regulation miracle, like the lame walking and lepers recovering. But maybe you underwent a type of reverse circumcision? Did the priest sew a bit of skin on - cover the wound, so to speak, when you were very young? You wouldn't remember that would you?"

"I can well recall my circumcision," Simon said.

I thought about this. Either he'd been done rather later than was common practice, or he had virtually total recall. I could have pursued that one, but I pressed on instead. "There is a custom in certain Afric tribes to the South and West of here," I said, "Where females have their parts sewn up. All the visible bits cut off and then the rest made whole, so to speak. What d'you reckon? Is it possible an over-zealous rabbi thought to do something like that with your mark of humanity, or mortality, as you call it?"

"Look not for explanations in mysteries and you will lead a more quiescent life," Simon said. I had to ask him what 'quiescent' meant though. Then he went off into another metaphor, instead of just offering a synonym. "There are two children in Tarsus joined at the rib who share one heart," he said. "Should we wonder how the ventricles pass the blood to the two sets of organs? Should we seek to explain the dynamics of their limbs as they walk, in a lifelong sack race of conjugation? Or should we praise the Lord for his husbandry? And for his ingenuity in conjoining two bodies with the Bostik of his love, rather than splitting those children with the sword of his might?"

"Well," I said, "It's a moot point. You're not prepared to run with the skin grafting theory then, I take it?"

"I am whole," he answered slowly, "But I am also blank. Who is to say if a mark makes a man any more than a man makes a mark? As to whether I am changed into the form I now occupy at the hand of doctor or rabbi, or whether it is a sign from God that I am in some way chosen, it is not for me to say, still less to ponder."

What an incurious man, I thought. If I was born flawed, or later discovered myself to be so, even if it was in terms of a flawless stretch of stomach, I'd certainly want to know who was responsible. I'd have had a word with my old man if my mother was unavailable for comment. I'd probably have avoided skimpy tops or bold bare-chested bravado too. I might have been tempted to get some dark dye and paint in a navel, with appropriate shadowing to suggest a bit of depth. I wouldn't have gone round praising the lord's husbandry, that's for certain.

"Don't they say we're not whole human beings till we find our other half?" I said. "Like we're sort of jigsaw pieces looking where to slot in?"

"But God's jigsaw puzzle has no end, no outer limits."

"No edge pieces, you mean?" I thought about the implications. "That would make it a lot harder to sort out, I guess." But I wasn't to be fobbed off with another of his nebulous metaphors that seemed to make things more concrete, but actually greased the slipperiness of what he was saying. "But what do you think about that, that we're only half of ourselves till we find the other half?"

"I think it's a trifle simplistic," Simon said. "But I suppose half a life is better than no breed."

"That's clever," I said. "Clever, but not much use, if you'll forgive me. What's so simplistic? I didn't necessarily mean another half as in a wife, or husband."

"Did you mean then that the missing piece is the work you must do, or the bonds you must make in life? You need to explain, my friend."

I thought for a moment. "Well, in your case, perhaps it's your god."

"A heretical point, I think," he replied. "God is no fraction, you know. He may be the whole puzzle, but he is not a mere part of it, to

61

return to your jigsaw puzzle trope."

"But didn't you climb up this mountain - well, pillar of rock really, isn't it? - to discover the missing pieces of your life? To get an aerial view of the big picture, sort of thing? To find where you fitted by isolating the black hole, to see the true shape of your selfhood? I'm sorry, I know this is harping on a bit, but I kind of think the jigsaw puzzle image, well, resonates ..."

"It will do. It's pleasantly non-agrarian, so it does make a change from sheep, and loaves and fishes, and prodigal sons, and that sort of thing."

"Well, I didn't use it just to be trendy," I complained. I was starting to wonder why I was getting the blame for us being locked in this particular metaphoric maze, when I was sure it was Simon who'd introduced the image in the first place. "I'm trying to get to the heart of the matter here, as it happens."

"Let us shift our ground," Simon said. "Metaphorically, of course. There is no great room for physical movement on this small platform, I fear."

I was well aware of that. I've got a touch of vertigo, to tell the truth, and I'd planted myself as near as I could to the centre of our little arena, to avoid having to look down the sheer sides of the outcrop.

"If God were to descend," he continued, "Would He not float down as if cushioned by the angels of the air?"

I nodded, though unsure where this paradescending deity was leading us.

"And would He not envelop a submissive and pious soul in his presence, his aura?"

"I guess that'd be about it, for the believer."

"Like the 4,999 pieces of a huge jigsaw puzzle gathering around that one poor, small, insignificant little piece?"

"Ah," I said. "I get it. The hole is the man, the polo mint is God?"

"Polo mints are pure and all encompassing, I presume?"

"Well, yes. They're white anyway. So, I suppose you're merely disputing my arithmetic? God is like 4,999 five-thousandths, not just a missing half?"

"That is somewhat literal, but you follow my meaning, I think."

"But if the hole is the blackness and God is the whiteness, how does that fit with people like me?" I said.

"You mean, because you are a black man?"

I'm dark, but I'm not that mad about being called black. "Differently-complexioned, I prefer ..." I said.

"Mmm, yes, well," Simon said, "That entails a different set of questions."

***

As you can imagine, I never got the article into print. It just didn't have the right zeitgeist, I guess. And they couldn't come up with a decent visual to go with it, in all probability. A ragged, shaggy-haired man crouched on a pillar, however long he's been there, is always going to be a speck in the distance, isn't he? I did try and win my editor round, but he just looked glazed as I ran through my notes. In fact, the only time he perked up a bit was when I mentioned the Siamese twins in Tarsus. I said I didn't fancy that job though. I'd heard there'd been some strange stuff on the road up there, some flashing light appearing or something. One of my colleagues is into all that UFO stuff, so I said I'd be happy for him to cover that one. I had a couple of other leads anyway. One was a story about a guy who'd organised some giant picnic for about five thousand people, but then the caterers had let him down. You always need a big event to give you focus for a good story. Some drama. I mean, Simon hadn't fallen off the pillar and plummeted to what should have been his certain death, but then been miraculously saved or anything, had he? In fact, as far as I know, he's still up there.

63

ORM'S EYE VIEW

My uncle Orm, or Ormin, as he was sometimes called, was a temperamental man given to outbursts of rage at the world, his own family, and society in general. Apparently he directed these outbursts in particular at a white mule he owned called Robin. But I do not know of these outbursts from first-hand experience, since I never met my uncle. That is unsurprising when you consider my own birthright of course. My father, so my mother assures me, was the prior of Bourne Abbey. Brother Walter was a good man, she says, though obviously prone to occasional lapses, such as the one that caused me to be brought into the world. As a man of God and an important figure at the abbey he could not possibly recognise me as his son, naturally, but he was Christian enough to provide my mother with certain means and to arrange for us to be removed from our Lincolnshire roots with some expediency. I was but a few weeks old at this time. Indeed, it is only since I have come to Stamford, whither I removed in the year of our Lord 1186, that I have been able to piece together something of my own history, and that of my father and his remarkable brother Orm.

You have to remember that England was quite different country at the beginning of this century. Far from the homogeneous place that it is now, it was a land of fractious churls and surly Danes and Norsemen only barely suppressed by our good Norman lords. It was a land where French and Latin competed with the garbled Wealesc tongue of the Celts and the mongrel dialects of the Angles, Jutes and Saxons. Furthermore it was a land where justice was meted out not by God's will, as it is now in our trials by combat, but through the arbitrary pronouncements of the dooms, or by-laws of each parish. No wonder that Orm felt he had to dedicate so much of his life (and good temper) inscribing his homilies: he was addressing a society splintered by so many tongues, as much as a society rent by war and cultural difference. Of course the writings are pretty hard to read. I've done little more than dip in myself, but I respect the fact that he was trying to offer his readers a value system as well as an exegesis of the good books. But it's not my uncle Orm's great work, *Ormulum*, that I want to talk about here. I want to set the record straight about his life, his vision and his mule Robin.

My uncle had one good eye, his right eye. The other, he always claimed, was put out in a fight he had the misfortune to get into with a villein who accosted him on the road to Lincoln. It is said that he gave a reasonably good account of himself in this confrontation, but nevertheless his antagonist managed to gouge out Orm's eye with a piece of rough ash. I'm not clear if this was a hand-made wooden blade the villein was wont to carry about his person, or a fortuitous weapon that happened to come to hand in the altercation. The offending article was never recovered, though the assailant was captured and brought to swift justice, God rest his soul. Orm's wounds were treated by an old hag dwelling in a hovel nearby, but thereafter, I am told, he never wore an eye patch. Instead, he allowed the world to see his disfigurement, and some disfigurement it must have been, for the skin grew over the cavity left by the torn out eyeball and gave him the seeming of a gruesome troll, or a kind of rather shorter Cyclops perhaps.

Perhaps Orm's vision was imperfect before this event, though he was a robust young man according to local legend. On the other hand, perhaps the loss of one eye was compensated for by an increased sharpness in the other senses, and perhaps there was no great detriment to his sight anyway. The Lord has seen fit to provide us with organs in pairs, for the most part, so that a degree of damage can be sustained to the human body without it ceasing to function altogether. I myself have but one ear, due to the deft sweep of a pagan's scimitar in the Holy Land, but I believe I hear as well as the next man. Certain it is, however, that Orm felt his loss sharply, for he was often heard imprecating the devil and the lower orders for his one-eyed state. And who would not sympathise with his position? He had risen from the level of scribe to the position of canon at Bourne Abbey, but he had always, from his earliest days, intended writing his great work *Ormulum*. Many men would hesitate before embarking upon such a task, with its inevitable inordinate strain upon the eyes, even if they possessed a full complement of those delicate organs, but my uncle was, as I say, robust.

It may be fanciful of me, but I like to believe that my uncle Orm's rather eccentric spelling owes something to his loss of his right eye. They say that a man may suffer double vision after a bad blow to the head. Could it not be that a man might suffer double vision when he has but a single eye, as that eye struggles to put the world into focus? This is to set aside the indubitable fact anyway that my uncle did suffer a bad blow to the cranium, prior to the act of gouging. Whatever, Orm insisted on doubling practically every consonant he came across in his writings. A waste of ink, you might think, but he got round that by the clever ploy of superscribing a number of the doubled consonants, like this - tur^tned^d. This does give the script a rather wavy feeling, it has to be said. You feel more like you're crossing the choppy Channel in a one man bark than harking to the sermons of SS Peter and Paul, or at the very least, like you're trying to read sheet music rather than plain text. He actually spelled his own name Orrmin, rather than Ormin, though as can be seen above, I give the latter spelling as the more elegant form. There are too many examples to list - *werre, farre, thatte*, the fair *Eddith* even. Eddith, my foot. Sounds not like the distaff side at all. Or should I write *disstaffe*. It looks so strange, doesn't it?

It may have been that Orm had some method in his mad^{d}ness. In addition to the business of doubling all his consonants, he obviously took considerable care over his vowels, which is, you may say, as it should be. Well, call me sloppy. Call me apathetic, or linguistically lazy - languorous I think I'd prefer though - but I just think an 'a' is an 'a'. I don't fret myself about its Norse or Anglo-Saxon origins and procrastinate about using an 'æ' instead in certain places. And I draw the line at '3' for 'y' or 'g'. If you started using numbers for letters where would you end up?

But it obviously wasn't a sudden whim that made Orm start spelling words in his own eccentric way. He must have put quite a bit of thought into it, because he went round changing lots of the words he'd written. Now he did this as we all do when we make an accidental mistake, by crossing out the word and writing in the changed version above, or in the margin. I suspect lots of people are like me, too cocksure, and don't think they're going to misspell anything and then don't leave enough space between lines or in the margin. I don't know how confident Orm was, or really how good his eyesight was, but he was clearly faced with this problem, so sometimes he used my strategy: he simply tried changing letters. Thus he changed his 'Þ' to a 'th' by squeezing in the extra letter and going over and over it with his pen. But from time to time he went to even greater efforts. He'd scrape off the ink from the hide or parchment with a keen knife blade before inserting the revised spelling. Now that's what I call pernickety, and it shows us that he took his writing damned seriously. Does the form and shape of things matter more than their meaning? Ask my lady Beth and she'll no doubt answer that outward appearance is everything, judging from the way she likes to spend my money on gowns and bonnets. But ask any sane man and he's like to tell you that substance is paramount, not style. And surely this should ever be truer of words than any other thing in God's creation?

Perhaps I should proffer an example. Did not our Saviour tell us that we should forgive our brothers seven times seventy times? He must have meant infinitely, for I, certes, can count not much above three hundred, with the most stubborn of wills, and 490, as I reckon it, is simply too large a number to mean anything but infinity. Now Christ did not worry about the style, still less the spelling, of his utterance. Heresy to think so. The substance was that we should be forgiving unto infinity. But Brother Wulfstan said to me only the other day that the actual remark made by our redeemer had been badly translated, and that what he said was 'seven *and* seventy times', which actually puts rather a different complexion on the matter of mercy. I can easily count to 77; it's a piece of oatmeal when you know your ciphering. That's the trouble with these translators who spend their lives trying to get everything right. And I'm afraid I have to say that the same applies to Orm and his particular school of orthographic pedantry: just because it sounds right and looks right on the parchment, doesn't mean you've caught the exact flavour of a man's thought.

Now I think about it, it was the same with the Pope and his sermon that time at Clermont. You have to picture it: there were several hundred of us, foot soldiers in the army of Christ, standing in the square in front of the blackened façade of the church of our Lady of Mercy. We were looking up at our holy father as he stood in his pomp on the steps in his dalmatic of white and gold thread. The sun was blazing and so were our hearts. Nothing could be heard but the cawing of a rook in the distance and the monotone of God's chosen priest as he intoned in classical Latin. I suppose I was taken in, like the rest of them, but he didn't actually *say*, "Go and exterminate everyone you bump into on the way to Jerusalem." His precise words were, "Rase the pagans." But who's to say he meant 'rase'? Given the benefit of hindsight, it's quite possible he might have meant 'raise', I see now. That could even mean 'put them on some sort of pedestal'. But this is it: there's Johnny Turk standing outside his whitewashed adobi, the glow of a Constantinople afternoon sun shining off the minarets of his temple, and he sees a troop of God's cavalry riding towards him. He must be thinking he's in for some exaltation from a crowd of cheering tourists with red crosses on their white vestments. Next thing he's got half a face and there's lances sticking through his womenfolk. Then, in the general mayhem, all he can hear, if he hasn't had an ear lobe already cut off as a trophy, is the screams of the wounded and dying and the cacophony of chickens and mules clucking and braying and running everywhere like rats fleeing from a rotten bark.

But the vision, nay, the memory, of that braying brings me back to the subject of Orm's white mule Robin. Like all beasts of its genus it was a stubborn creature. I say this because I have heard as much from those old folk who still survive and remember it and its dealings with my uncle Orm. I feel free to vouchsafe its obdurate nature because I have owned a mule myself, and I am therefore in a position to recognise that, of all God's creation, a mule is the stubbornest, most cantankerous animal in the entire bestiary. But my own mule Daisy, I believe, was a model of passivity and good will compared to Orm's single-minded beast of burden. The particular pig-headedness of the mule Robin may be accounted for by the cataracts that the creature suffered in both eyes. It was blind as fog from quite an early age, apparently, and, though its optical limitations were nothing to do with its owner, it seemed to take exception to my uncle's ever wanting it to move from the spot where it had last came to rest. Perhaps it is discomforting to have to move when you cannot see even a blurred outline of where you are supposed to be going. Perhaps I do the creature too much credit, however. Uncle Orm only infrequently left the abbey, consumed as he was with trying to get the metre right in his homilies and the spelling right (or wrong, to my mind) in his fearful *Ormulum*. And then he only tended to leave its confines in order to take a basket of crab apples from the luxuriant orchards in the grounds to an old crone in the nearby hamlet. Or perhaps he'd wander down from the abbey to help gather the danegeld from a local hide. Now, it is self-evident that a mule exists to carry a man, or whatever burdens a man may choose to heap upon it. It is unfair, accordingly, to suggest that cataracts of the eyes are any sort of excuse for immobility.

The older people hereabouts remember Orm's white face and clenched fists as, on one of these infrequent occasions, he endeavoured to get the mule to undertake the short stroll down from the abbey to the cottage of one or other of the cotarii or servii. They recall his booming voice fluking up an octave or two to a falsetto beseeching as he alternately implored with and cajoled the animal to get moving.

I want to relate what happened on one of these occasions. It was a sunny day in late June, I am told. Birds were chirping and the early dew was still sparkling on the greensward. Uncle Orm had a wicker basket containing a few punnets of the choicest strawberries, which he was intending to take, as an act of pure altruism, to a young woman of the parish who had been newly widowed. He lifted a skirt of his mid-brown cassock and attempted to mount the pertinacious mule. The beast gave out the most lamentable braying sound and took a pace to one side, causing Orm to topple forward into its flank. The strawberries were scattered hither and thither like seed on the stony ground, so it was natural that Orm felt he had to administer some retribution to the obstinate mule. He picked up his ash rod, which had been cast from him by the misadventurous attempt at mounting, and belaboured the beast with it for a while. The mule flinched and brayed but did not move an ell from where it stood, as if it were a piece of statuary Then, when my uncle's arm began to ache and he was forced to desist from his castigations, the animal turned its head slowly to face its taskmaster. Its two opaque, cataracted eyes stared balefully at Orm's one eye, though of course no beams could be emitted from those veiled brown orbs, and more than likely Orm's eye was narrowed to a bow slit by his brow-furrowing concentration on chastisement of the beast. This face-off might have lasted longer than it did, but the two antagonists were suddenly hailed by a high pitched voice.

"O sir, desist!" It was the voice of a young girl.

Orm spun round and saw that the person who had the temerity to call out to him in this manner was a slip of a lass no more than fifteen years of age. She was dressed in a grey smock that barely came down to her grubby knees. Her face and hands were equally grimy and her hair was a bird's nest of tangled auburn straw.

"Why," my uncle said in some astonishment. "Who are you that dare rebuke me so?" His words are the exact ones, it is avouched to me, and they might seem harsh, but there was apparently an unwonted tenderness in Orm's tones. Perhaps it was the girl's pert manner that suddenly fired in him this modulation.

"My name is Constance," the girl said. "And yours is Ormin, I know, though of course we have never spoken. I am well acquainted with Robin, that poor blind beast, however, and he does not deserve such treatment at your hands."

"Whose child are you?" Orm asked the girl.

"I am nobody's child. I am nigh a woman. I will be sixteen years of age next Lentilmas."

Orm may have smiled; my testimony is unclear on the matter, but what is certain is that he took the young girl by the elbow and led her round to the other side of the still immutable mule. "You say you know this creature," he said to her. "Whence comes this acquaintance?"

She told him how she had from an early age been sent by her

mother to the abbey to do odd chores in the stables, and how she had sometimes been allowed to take out the animals' bedding straw. It was a great boon in her house, she maintained, for it could be employed in stuffing her parents' palliasse.

"You mean you sleep on straw that has been deemed no longer worthy for our mules?" Orm asked.

"No, not me, sir. My parents. I make my rest on a length of wood."

Perhaps it was at this point that Orm felt for the first time that he had not taken enough care of such things as the plight of the servii. He may have come to a Pauline realisation that he had been too deeply engrossed in his studies and writings to note that the peasants were, after all, in a pretty poor state. All through the period of The Anarchy, indeed since coming across The Black Book of Peterborough, Orm had neglected to question social issues. I know for a fact myself that in those days your average serf was obliged to pay a 30p fee to his lord to become worthy of his hide, but I guess Orm was too dedicated to matters of the soul for such matters of economics. Nevertheless, at this moment his compassion for the serving classes was roused to such a state that he felt compelled to lay one bony hand on the girl's bare shoulder and to run his fingers through her thick straw hair. Simultaneously he let his cassocked knee nestle against her thin shank for a moment, before allowing it to move up and grind into her bony groin.

"If you want poor Robin to move, you must offer the carrot as well as the stick," the girl said, deftly sidestepping Orm's knee and patting down the thin fabric of her ruffled smock.

"What do you mean, you piece of impudence?" Orm retorted. "This is the season of the juicy strawberry and the tender *phaseolus multiflorus*, or scarlet runner bean, as you probably know it, not the season of the carrot."

"I was speaking in figures," the damsel replied, obviously deaf to the doubling of her interlocutor's consonants. "You must persuade your blind beast to want to move. Here, let me show you." With this she put her moist pink lips nigh the mule's muzzle and blew softly into its nosethirles. The beast exhaled a huge sigh and flicked a hairy ear towards its new mentor. She held out a hand and let the mule unleash a coarse and lengthy tongue that rasped against her tiny, well shaped palm. "He likes the salt," she said simply. Then she took the bridle and stepped backwards, smiling as the animal lurched forward a pace, reaching out its huge snout to taste of her flesh once more.

Orm stooped to gather up as much of his fallen fruit as he could before hurrying after the girl and her new charge as they plodded down the path to the village. In truth it was but a pleasant amble, but Orm was gasping for breath and bathed in sweat when they reached the fork in the track where the dusty road to the hamlet meets the grassy path to the nearby wood.

"There is a special clover in a grassy knoll I know of in yonder wood," she said. "I think poor Robin would love to graze at it."

Perhaps Orm feared he was about to be traduced by the starveling maiden. He might have hazarded that her bigger, better fed brothers were stationed behind the twisted boles of the oaks in that darkened place, waiting to waylay him and put out his one remaining good eye. Their prize would not have been a great one, for Orm wore only one good gold chain, eschewing other vanities, as is only right and proper for the priesthood. For whatever reason anyway, he hesitated, so it is said, before following the maiden into the dappled copse. But follow her he did, and perhaps with a tremulous heart. Unfortunately what ensued is a matter of conjecture, but I do know that Orm began to write love poems from that day. They spoke of the sensuous passions that a man may feel when he is stirred by a vision of pulchritude. They went on a bit about Abelard and his love too, and how his love was as pure as snow, as bleached as the desert sands, and a few things like that, but I tended to skip some sections, to tell the truth. Those writings are all destroyed now, of course, for it was my duty to God and my family to preserve only those texts and testimonies that exalt my forebears. Hence the *Ormulum* is still around. But I was privileged to be the one man on earth to read those verses. Thus it is that I am sure it was the gamine Constance who sparked my uncle's heart and caused his human love to flow as it did, secretly but enduringly from that time. As a consequence I think I can pretty well guess what happened in the wood that sunlit day. It was probably much like this:

The sinuous path led to a small clearing where thyme and lavender blew and the air was thick with the reek of cow parsley and oregano. Robin's stiff-legged gait might have quickened at the prospect of the promised dense green clover. Constance must have let slip the bridle and let the beast wander to where it could snuffle and gorge on the chewy leaves. In my mind's eye I see her reaching up to a low-lying branch with her slender, brown-mottled arms and swinging once or twice in untrammelled innocent pleasure. In an old manuscript I once saw there is an engraving of Eve in such a disposition, a dangling leaf demurely covering her parts, but her milk white breasts exposed in her primordial state of bliss. Adam is looking on benignly, unashamed and unprovoked. It would be nice to suppose that Orm could have looked on in much the same manner, but Constance was no Eve. She was a lot skinnier for one thing, for she was a mere adolescent, not a voluptuous woman as the mother of our race must have been. But also she was a village hoyden. She must have encountered men's rapine pleasures, if only at the hands of her brothers and uncles. It is well known that the servii have never held incest as much of a sin, and it is to be supposed that they still, as a matter of course, regularly deflower the family virgins at the point of puberty.

What could Orm have thought, as he saw her swaying from a branch like a Barbary ape? He could only possibly have reflected that she meant to entice him by these antics. Gentleman that he was, however, I am sure he held out his thicker arms and gently let her drop to the ground in his embrace. She may have tripped and fallen, causing my uncle to stumble too. They would have laughed at their clumsiness as they tried to disentangle their knotted limbs. She may have ripped her already threadbare smock on a twig of thorn and exposed a slender shank, or a soft cupola of her young maid's bosom. Her cheeks may have glowed carnation pink from her exertions. Orm's breathing was already stertorous, we must recall, from the unwonted physical activity of traipsing down the hill, rather than riding upon Robin's back.

73

From what I may judge from my uncle's verses, their lips must have met at about this point. It may have been an accidental brushing as they both leaned forward to rise to their feet. On the other hand it may well have been that the strumpet deliberately sought to seduce this man of the cloth, who knew so little of matters of the flesh. They kissed, I'm certain. It is an indisputable fact that no man of blood and bile, lymph and choler, can restrain himself when thrust into an embrace with a girl who is eager and nubile, fresh-faced (albeit perhaps a bit grubby) and fertile. How then could Orm refrain? There was her pudendum, pert and proud; there were her bubs, as yet buds, but perfectly formed; above all, there were the cheeks of her bottom, rounded and white and alabaster smooth. I am sure he prayed to Almighty God for guidance and release, but Orm was, though a scholar, a scribe, a canon, and a man of God, nevertheless a man. The truth has to be told: Orm reached out and grasped the girl's tiny hand and placed it on his organ. She responded enthusiastically, but with perhaps too little skill, for my uncle could not respond as a man should do. His member was, of course, unused to such manipulation. It was plainly shrivelled and weak from years of starvation, for Orm's brain had demanded for decades all the blood and vitality that the vessels of his body could supply. Who would stoop to blame a man of Orm's lofty position when he could not rise to the occasion, therefore? He cast aside her flimsy fingers and jumped up in self-mortifying rage. He strode and hither and thither in the woody den looking for a sign from his Lord and for some birch twigs to flagellate himself. Then all at once he recognised a special misericord and, gathering together a small number of pliable twigs, he returned to where Constance was crouching. She may have looked demure, but in all probability she must have appeared to my uncle as a homunculus gloating triumphantly at the humiliation she had visited upon her master. He did what he had to do.

He threw her upon her stomach, pulled up her ragged skirt to expose the lily globes of her buttocks, and then he began to belabour her with his makeshift paddle. Her cheeks blossomed fuchsia pink at each stroke. She yelped with gratification at the tickling sensation, disturbing the nesting wood pigeons, no doubt, from their leafy arbour above. The blind mule Robin turned his head for a moment from his clover feast to attend to the screams of delight. But the girl was a mere pagan, and unpractised in Christian arts such as humbling oneself before God. She tried to leap up and scamper away, like a forest fawn startled by its shadow in the dappled glade. My uncle restrained her, however, and redoubled his playful blows. He may have drawn a few beads of blood, but these were as blissful stigmata, he knew. Anyway, the price was a small one for the delectation he felt as his member remembered its youthful vigour and rose in his cassock like a morning lark.

The beating lasted some forty minutes. At last the girl was sated and my uncle's arms were too sore to continue. He lay back, spent and exalted. Now it is at this point that I cannot be certain of consequent events. The villagers remember that when the trollop returned to her hovel she was in an ecstatic daze, like some anchorite or dervish purified and entranced by devotion. Thereafter they swear she was little more than an imbecile roving the edges of the wood for faggots of wood and wild mushrooms. They assumed she had been taken by the devil and turned to a witch, but they were kindly people and refused to have her burnt. One old crone insisted the girl had been attacked and had her head stove in by a passing ragamuffin, but though this is as implausible as a day without sun or a night without stars, there may be a sort of truth in the crone's story. I believe that what happened was this: as Orm lay back in the grass the girl crawled away to prevent Robin, the mule, from straying too far. Blind as he was, the beast could not know her intentions were merely to attach once more his bridle. He must have lashed out with his hind foot and caught her a glancing blow above the temple. This would explain her insanity from that day. Everyone knows that mules are pertinaceous creatures and need to be approached from behind with consummate care and discretion. The animal's cupidity would have made it believe that its repast was about to be disturbed, and it may have been as much in rage as fright that it kicked out with its hoof as it must have done.

But it is not simply knowledge of mules that makes me so certain that this is what happened. As I mentioned, Orm wrote copious poetry from this day onwards and described his manly emotions in unvarnished language and fulsome detail. He was not a man to be untruthful to himself about himself, and his love for mankind and all the natural world grew fuller as each day passed. He never, as I swear, laid rod to Robin again. On the contrary, though he could have punished the beast for its act of folly and head-banging, he treated the dumb creature henceforward with increased love and gentleness. He went every morning after matins and every evening before mass to the stable to attend to its smallest desire. By his own hand he laid fresh bedding straw each week. He would dangle a fat juicy carrot before its musk-smelling muzzle. He would pat its hindquarters and stroke its tenderest parts in a manner that might have moved even the good saint from Assissi. In short, he treated the mule as a brother might a younger sister, or an uncle a niece. He even wrote poems 'To Robin'.

But this is where the business of Orm's orthography comes in. I have already related his practice of superscribing his doubled consonants. In one of the poems he makes it clear how he stumbled upon this device for the *Ormulum*. The handwriting is not perfectly clear, but the gist is that he became obsessed with "little 'r's in the air". In an epigraph to one of the poems dedicated to his mule he demonstrates how his love for his fellow creatures and his linguistic inventiveness are entwined and enmeshed, like briars in a dingle. The words are Latin, of course, but this is what he wrote:

Mule est hominis amorata

It's an astonishing piece of honesty, as I take it. Woman is, of course, the love of mankind, but the little 'r' clearly stands for Robin, the mule too, which proves my uncle's humanity and humility before all that God has created and blessed.

THE PRESIDENT'S MISSING BRAIN

It's a problem. For over five hundred years now we've been working on cryogenic techniques so that our most important citizens can be revitalised. We've got a huge stock of them: artists and martyrs, musicians and politicians, Victorians and historians, philosophers and officers, thinkers and drinkers, movers and groovers, breakers and shakers They're all kept in pristine formaldehyde in row upon row of plasti-tombs on Delta 4, waiting for our cryo-technicians to thaw them out and get them re-functioning for the good of society. The irony is, the one thing we need to begin the re-birthing programme is lost to us. But it was the president's own idea to plant the access code in his own floating brain, so for once we can't blame the scientists.

I suppose you could argue that we should have had a back-up device, but that would have meant trying to store zillions of Brian Waves somewhere in the physical environment. Since we abandoned the slow-moving computer technology of the twenty first century, and adopted Cerebration Information Transfer, we had no need for vast external data storage facilities, however. It was just as well, since the heat wave of 2323 would have melted all the plastic software, I suppose. It's hard enough trying to imagine all those clumsy three and three quarter inch disks they used to have, but before that they had huge things – books – and they had to be kept in enormous buildings. Naturally, we've kept some of that beautiful old architecture, like the Smithsonian Institute and the National Archive in Western America, and The Tate Ancient and the British Library in Middle America, but it's amazing to think that people in the Modern Age used to keep all their wordefacts in huge stone edifices, isn't it? How could they share knowledge, when only one person could read a book at any one time? Obviously it would have been nice to keep the contents of those grand old buildings, but paper only had a half-life of two stigmons and you've got to recognise that The Great Burning of

2480 was a fantastic occasion. Anyway, hardly anybody can understand Early Amerispeak anymore, so it wasn't a great loss, as most people agree. Perhaps it's a quaint notion, but I quite like it that you can still get some idea of life in those days by looking at the leather-look polycarbonate dummy books stuck to the walls in those places.

The move to cerebral information storage was plainly a big step towards the eradication of data crime, but it seems you can never have a foolproof system. Successive generations have tried all sorts of means to guarantee the security of important ideas and information – you can go all the way back to keys, through card chips and up to Neuro-Securo to see that – but something's always bound to go wrong. And that's where we get to the story of President Brian's big brain.

It was a hot day, I remember, in the autumn of 2463 that I heard about our leader's sad demise. He'd been unwell for some time, though he was only a hundred and eighty years old, but it still came as a shock when everybody received the brainwave that the president had died. I said to Simon, my great-great grandson, "This is a tragic day for uskind and no mistake." Simon was having intra-sex at the time and he was only half attending, but he gave me the old no-smile and said, "I guess President Brian wasn't immortal after all." Such profundities from the mouths of thirty-one year olds! I mentally patted him on the head and returned a lingering no-smile. "Perhaps Mistress Jacky Lean will take over, till the cryos can get him back functioning," I said. "Maybe," Simon answered. "But they'll have to prise her out of the Thinning Centre first."

We thought about it together. Simon deflected off onto another intra-orgasm though and I was left to mark the seriousness of the moment with a short Coke, my eyes lifted to the firmament in due respect for the passing of the president.

Later, everybody remembered what they had been doing or un-doing at the moment of the mental announcement. Robinson, my neighbour, said he was ironing his underwear and he left the laser on too long and burnt his uni-bra. Ronaldo, who works in the next office to me at the Training Shoe Development Corporation of East America, said he was imagining some new sphere music and it came to him in a flash, just as he percepted the news. He's recorded the music now and thought it right across the world. He even called it "Coverture for Brian', as a mark of his respect. He decided not to give up his hour job at TrainerCorp though. He said it keeps his feet on the ground, but I know he's serious about it really and he's the sort of guy to recognise it's good to contribute to society in some fundamental way.

They ran a questionnaire on the thinkovision the other day about the Day of the Death, as that humid November day came to be called. 63% of respondents claimed they knew where they were at the moment Brian died. A further 29% said they knew where everybody else was, but had forgotten their own precise location. That only left 8% of the entire population, and most of them were in anti-think cells, or too busy preparing for the Anti-Democracy Protest in Southern State later that November.

So, as I say, I can recall exactly where I was and what I was doing, which is surprising when you consider that we all presumed that Brian would be back in office as soon as was cryogenetically possible. Well, I say all of us, but I can remember feeling some despair myself. I don't know, it almost seems to me now that I must have had some premonition that they'd lose his brain, and with it the access codes to human revivification. It was two years before the loss, or theft, came to light, however. Most people blame Brian's brother, Bobbly, but I'm not so sure. But this is what I do know, and I know it better then reportingly, I can assure you.

The President died of a severe nose-over. It happens from time to time, people snort too much and they wake up with a terrible nasal ache. Cases get reported where really heavy users destroy that bit of bone between the nostrils, the septum, I believe it's called. But they don't die. As I mentioned, the president wasn't in perfect health; he'd had a few spells in The Monroe Venereal Clinic in his later years, for instance. But you'd think all those presidential medicos would have had an instant cure for morning after ailments, wouldn't you? Not so, it seems. Whatever, he expired peacefully in the Big Bed. Vice-president Johnson immediately ordered in the brain removers and everything looked like it would turn out fine. The brain was put in a metal container and labelled 'gross material', for the sake of decency obviously, and placed in a footlocker in the Black House. Now, only Bobbly and VP Johnson had access to this double sealed container, so you might think it was an open and shut case. Literally, so to speak. But the Black House employed several hundred aides and customer safety personnel, so maybe it's conceivable that one of them could have thought the access code and removed the brain. Why though? Brian had been a good leader for several decades, despite a few scandals involving Hollygood actresses and the odd intern or two. He was a handsome man, over seven feet tall, with a fine head of ungrey hair that he kept way into his hundred and fifties. But it wasn't his physical attractions that excited the ladies, or impressed the public; it was his brain, of course. It was a huge specimen, the shape of an American football and over a foot in diameter, and it was packed with information and ideas, both pragmatic and profound. Obviously, all presidents and TrainerCorp chief executives have to have a replica of their cerebrum made as soon as they are first appointed, and it was this replica that was shown on thinkovision shortly after Brian died. It was a moving experience, sitting in a McBud fast drink outlet and watching everyone gasp at the size of the thing. Women and childroids were weeping like gum trees. One woman had an instant intra-orgasm as she saw the deep canals of the left hemisphere gouged into the unearthly landscape of that mighty organ. Another woman turned to her manwife and slapped him upside his head, with the words "Look at that, pea brain, and suffer!" I have to admit I underwent a few pangs of brain envy myself. But nobody could feel so jealous that they'd actually steal the big brain, could they?

No. I don't believe it was an aide or a security goon that removed the gross material from the footlocker. However impressive it was in terms of size, it was what was inside that was the important thing. And of course the main thing that was inside was the access code for us to revitalise all our frozen heroes. Imagine, Ghengis Disney, Dwight McDuck, the Pepsi brothers – all the great innovators of the last two centuries. We could even have gone back further, for we had the frozen organs of many of the profound thinkers of the twenty first and twenty

80

second centuries cryo-stored. With the accessing technology almost within sight we could have plundered the think streams of the reconstituted plasti-brains of people like Chelsea Clinton, or the other co-founders of the Complete States of America. Some experts claimed that we could have gone the whole five metres and thought the works of the ancients, like Shakespeare, Ella Wheeler Wilcox, Bach, Presley and Po Na Na, into an empty brain. Then it would have been a relatively simple matter to produce completely new and relevance-updated masterpieces of literature and music. We could have had *Romeo and Juliet* set to the rhythms of classic Coke jingles and really transformed today's Pre-Post-Praeter-Anti-Modernist cultural forms.

I'm convinced the box with the brain went missing within hours of Brian's tempo-demise. It could have been a simple mistake – a goon carrying the metal box down to the sub-basement storage lockers in the Black House might simply have slipped on the descendovator and dropped it. The brain could have rolled out of the box and cracked against a wall and split into its two hemispheres, like the meatball on top of old spaghetti in the ancient myth. What would the goon have done? He would have tried to slap the two halves together, but in so doing he might have got a finger caught in one of the subcutaneous grooves. I can imagine a big redfaced security guard yelping with pain as he finds his little finger wedged in the President's vein of Galen, or even his sagittal sinus. He'd drop the two halves – remember, they were the size and weight of two grey house bricks – and then what would he see on the plasti-floor in front of him? A ghastly spaghetti of basal ganglia, half a cerebellum, various shards of hindbrain and midbrain, five hundred billion neurons scattered down the steel grey corridor like styrofoam pellets from a torn cushion. Nobody could put that lot back together, not a neuro surgeon, not a pan-universe jigsaw champion, not even an assembly of all of history's kings' horses (whatever they are) and kings' men. There'd be nothing to do but sweep up the whole shebang and dump it down the nearest shit chute. The President's life, memories, thoughts and the access code to all our ancestors' lives, memories and thoughts would end up in a dumpster in an alley outside the Black House. What I can't conceive though is what the guard would have done

81

to make up the weight in the metal box. You've got to remember that a normal person's brain weighs 1400 grams, but Brian's broca's area alone would have weighed at least that much. The whole brain would have come in at about 6000 grams, which is roughly the weight of the organ of an elephant from the early period. Now there is an account of a one-footed customer safety officer working at the Black House in the mid-sixties, which I saw once in the register of personnel on Thinkovision's History Channel. It's far-fetched, but it's possible that, in an act of extreme desperation, this goon might have cut off his own foot and placed it in the box. I don't believe it though. Even with a size thirteen shoe still on, it wouldn't have weighed the right amount. No. I discount the BrainDrop theory on two counts. Firstly, there are no reports that the one-footed guard failed to report for duty around that time, and surely he would have had to take some time off work to undergo surgery, even if it was meditational self-medicine he used to seal and heal the amputated foot. Secondly, Brother Bobbly would doubtless have checked the contents of the box before finally sealing it up in the footlocker. He'd hardly have appeared on thinkovision the next day with that no-smile of grief at his brother's brain death that moved the people so much, if it was a guard's foot he'd sepulchred, would he?

I think it was altogether different. But I didn't come to the conclusions I presently hold until a while after the autumn of 2463. It was three years later, to be precise, that I finally realised what must have happened in the basement corridors of the Black House. But by that time I'd met Jim Barrackson, of course, and I'd come to TrainerCorp to work.

I don't want to blow my own trumpet, but I regard myself as a pretty normal de-unreconstructed twenty-fifth-century male. I work a five-hour week like anyone else; I'm happily unmarried to my seventh unwife; I've got three childroids with her and sixty or seventy grandchildroids by previous tempo-lovers. All in all I'm a normal happy de-married man. As for my hobbies, I do a bit of gardening, though there never seems enough time for that, and of course I play thinkball with the lads on a Saturday. I've always regarded myself as a moderate man too: I Coke it up a few times a week, but no more than the next person, and I rarely do intra-sex unless Miriam, my present unwife, is away for a day or two on a lunar-shopping trip or something like that. But then I got the job at TrainerCorp as a quality advisor and my immediate boss turned out to be Jim Barrackson. We hit it off straight away as workbuds and as friends, and it seemed natural when, a couple of weeks later, he invited me and Miriam to his flatlet. Miriam couldn't come, because it was one of her lypo-weekends, so I went alone. That was the day two things happened to me that changed my life: I began to puzzle over the president's missing brain and I met Eva, Jim's great-granddaughter.

She was fifteen years old, so only newly sprouted in terms of her chest area, but I was dumbstruck by her beauty, her poise and the euphony of her thoughts. We started cross-thinking and inter-laughing as if we'd known each other for years. Jim only left us alone for a few minutes as he went to the micro-kitchen to prepare some home brewed McBud – DIY was a craze in the sixties – but I think he must have seen what was going on the minute he came back in the room. He handed me a plastic of McBud with a genuine smile and he said, "She's a beautiful girl, isn't she? Got a brain the size of a dolphin's too."

I knew I'd been struck by the thunderbolt, but I was trying not to show it. Useless. I was like a man coming out of the swimmo-shower pretending to be dry. As for Eva, she'd already pre-come half a dozen times. There was nothing she could do but try to no-smile nervously and cross her legs like a French plait to stop any further embarrassments. Jim looked at us ironically. "I may have to pop back out to do some more home brewing soon, but there's a matter I'd like to bring up with our guest first," he said. "Eva, if you wouldn't mind?" She jumped up quickly, and somewhat leakily, and went to her room, but not without a quick cross-think in my direction. It was only a micro-cerebration, but it made me hornier than a herd of rhinos, I can tell you.

"Listen," Jim said to me, "I've been working on something that you might be interested in."

I took a pull at my warm McBud and said I was all lobes. He looked gratified. Then, lowering his voice, he began his story. "I used to live in

83

Southern State," he said, "And I guess you know something of what that's like."

I knew, but only from Thinkovision. "The men all have tattoos and the women all weigh three hundred pounds?" I offered.

"Well, yes, of course, but I mean there's a way of doing things in those parts that's kind of different from the way people operate here in British Middle America."

I gestured for him to go on.

"Well, for one thing, folks back there still practice disorganised religion. You know that?"

I said I did, though it's fairly incomprehensible to me how people can still believe in the myths of post-Darwinianism, when for several decades Berkstein's theories have been shown to be two hundred percent infallible and most normal citizens understand that there is only one true Brain-God. "Yes, but what about it?" I said.

"Well, President Brian originally came from Southern State and he was campaigning in his home town just before he came up for his twenty first term. That was shortly before he died, wasn't it?" I decided not to interrupt further but let him get on with what he so desperately wanted to tell me. I nodded.

"In Southern State they cling to outmoded customs and beliefs, like the sanctity of the body and the one site of the brain, you know? Now listen, this is strictly confidential stuff, but I've got evidence that the President underwent surgery while he was on that campaign trail. It was supposed to be simply a case of a trapped neuron, but I believe Brian had his whole brain removed. You can try and rationalise all this, but I think some pre-post-radical madman of a doctor took out the brain to prevent it being transplanted into a new body when the president reached full term. That would explain how the President made no significant policy decisions when he returned to the Black House. I know it was only a few months later that he died, but a vigorous, mentally active man like Brian would normally have passed a whole raft of new legislation in that time, don't you think? He would have come up with a

84

scheme to de-increase taxes, for one thing. I mean, he did that every few weeks as a matter of course anyway, but there's nothing like that on the statute screens. In fact, if you examine the acts passed in those few months he did nothing but outlaw anti-Coke campaigning and reinstate the ultra-sex channel on Thinkovision. Do you see what I'm getting at here? Brian was carrying a new brain, probably taken from some hairy, tattooed roadster who'd died in a highway pile-up."

"But, if Southerners believe in the one site of the brain, as you say, whoever conducted the transplant would have been contravening his own beliefs in performing the lobotomy in the first place, wouldn't he?"

"Ah, there's the rub, my friend. He would have done it as the lesser of two evils. Obviously, when it was Brian's time to pass, this madman knew the brain would be removed and stored till a new human vessel could be found for it. Better to take it out himself, he must have reasoned, so that its one site sanctity would be secured, than have the thing publicly exhibited, ogled and orgasmed to, and then jammed into the next president-elect's cranium."

"But everyone saw the brain on Thinkovision anyway," I said.

Jim looked at me as if I was three, and had just spilled Coke on the plasti-floor. "Everyone saw the replica," he said softly. "Only Brian's brother Bobbly, and possibly Vice-president Johnson ever saw the real thing."

"But what about the surgeon who removed the brain after Brian had died?" I said. "He must have seen it. He would have noticed if it had been smaller than expected, wouldn't he? I take it that Southern Staters have brains no bigger than sprouts, if what you say about their primitive beliefs is really true."

"I admit that's a mystery," Jim said. "But it was a certain Dr Roswell who performed the surgery and he's dead now. Died in a heli-tragedy not long after the event, as a matter of fact."

I'd heard of this air disaster but never made any connection with the President. An eminent doctor had died on a routine golf mission. As the greatest of the twentieth century writers puts it: 'So it goes.' I must have sighed out loud. "So, there's no one alive to ratify if it was the President's brain that was put in the metal container in the first place?"

"Exactly. But Bobbly wouldn't just have had the brain placed in storage without taking one last peek, would he? The truth is, he never said a word. Remember, it was two years later that they announced that the brain had disappeared from the box. Everyone was waiting for the last revivification protocols to be finalised, so that the access codes could be released from Brian's fiber tracts. It was only then that they discovered the box was empty, wasn't it?"

Previously, though the affair of the missing organ was a long running item on Thinkovision News, I'd never given much thought to the metal container itself. Like everyone else, I was too shocked to consider weights and measures. Now, I asked the obvious question. "If Bobbly saw it wasn't his brother's brain and he took the roadster's brain out to hush things up, what did he put back inside?" Suddenly a host of other questions sprang into my feverish mind. "Why was it never announced that there was something else in the box? And if the box was empty, how come no one ever noticed? Wasn't it moved from the basement of the Black House to the family memorial home? It must have been far too light for it not to have come to someone's attention."

"Well," Jim said, "This is my theory. Bobbly saw that the brain wasn't the right one, so he removed the offending matter. But he would have had to put something back in, as you rightly note, or he would have been accused of tampering with state property. But whatever he replaced it with was bound to put him right in the frame anyway. That is, unless he put in something degradable. Naturally, he would still have been taking quite a risk, for he couldn't know how long it would be before the box was re-opened for the access codes. It would have to be something that was about the right weight, but would disappear comparatively quickly." I was given a no-smile that chilled me.

"You mean, not necessarily something that would bio-degrade, which might take too long, but something that would just evaporate away?"

"Precisely. Now what would that be?"

86

I tried to remember the periodic chart from pre-elementary university days. "Zircon?" I ventured. "No, that's inert, isn't it? But what about gaseous lead?"

"Too aromatic," Jim said.

Triumphantly, "Water!" I exclaimed. "There's no odour and it would simply evaporate after a few days and there'd be no trace left."

"Good, but you've got to recall the size of that container. It was only slightly larger than the brain itself. Now water is pretty dense, I grant you, but if you imagine a plastic filled with water, how heavy is that?"

Jim saw me doing a mental calculation that involved me holding out one hand and weighing an imaginary vessel in it.

"Let me tell you, no more than a thousand grams. The metal box was about the size of a Coke hip flask, perhaps a bit bigger, so water would have been too light."

I plainly looked disappointed.

"But, don't you see," Jim cried, "It must have been heavy water!"

"You mean radioactive heavy water?"

"Of course, radioactive, what other heavy water is there?"

"But Bobbly would have needed a geigerman to do that for him, wouldn't he? Would he have let someone else like that in on the scheme?"

"He may well have had his own heavy water supply. Remember, this was back in the days before global watering. It's my conviction that he measured out six kilos of heavy duty heavy water, sypho-poured it in, sealed up the box with the presidential seal and left it to dry up and completely disappear. No brain, no evidence, no crime."

"But there was still a brain. The roadster's. What would he have done with that? I can't imagine it's all that easy to dispose of incriminating evidence in the Black House. Think-cameras everywhere, shit chutes on permanent video-scan, no one you'd ever dare trust."

"I haven't worked that one out yet. I'm still trying to uncover a lot of things, not least if VP Johnson had any significant part to play in the nefarious business, but you've got to admit that it explains a lot, doesn't it? Like the subsequent banning of home-use heavy water, like maybe the fact that Bobbly was assassinated only eighteen months later. What do you think?"

I said I needed time to take in the enormity of what he'd been telling me. I said I'd like to think about it and maybe come back and talk it over a few days later. I was profoundly affected by everything he was suggesting. I was also profoundly hoping that next time I might get the chance to spend some more time with his great-granddaughter Eva.

I went home in a new thoughtful mood that day and, after smoking a herbal viagra in the swimmo-shower and intra-sexing myself a couple of times, I sat down to second breakfast with a new sense of mission in life. As I said before, I'd always regarded myself as a fairly normal type of guy, but now it was almost as if I'd been revivified. I was embarked upon a crusade, like those knights of bolden times. Indeed, I might have been feeling the same emotions they did as they set off to look for the holy gravy all those centuries ago.

I went back to Jim Barrackson's flatlet two days later and we scanned up our thoughts on his screen. There was no need for verbal communication this time because Jim had set up a cerebro-interface in order to speed things up and to save on vocal cord wastage. I was glad about that, because talk is tiring and a poor means of communicating anyway. Also, it meant that Jim was concentrating on what I was thinking about President Brian, and not tuning into my lascivious supra-thoughts about Eva. After an hour or two he said he needed a Coke break and he left me alone. As I somehow knew she would, Eva appeared at my side within a few moments.

"Great grandpops said you might like a mutuo-sex break, because you've both been working so hard at your little conspiracy problem," she smiled.

88

"I don't know about *little* problem," I said, "But I'm certainly up for a quickie, if you've got a couple of minutes. D'you want to do it regularly, or would you like us to get things started with a bit of verb-play first?"

"You're quite an old fashioned man, aren't you? she said, reaching out and touching my ear lobe and caressing it with a thumb and forefinger. "I think it'd be kind of fun to talk a little, if you've got the time. Would you mind that?"

"I rather think I would like it," I said. "Miriam, my unwife, doesn't really understand me, you know."

"I'll try then," she murmured nuzzling at my ear. "Everybody needs a woman for a pillow, after all, and I'm not due for my flute lesson for a while. And great-grandpops asked me to entertain you for twenty minutes while he refuels."

I'm sure I don't need to go into unnecessary detail, but we spent that twenty minutes in utter de-adulterated pleasure. I told her about my time as an amateur astronaut and the time I'd pre-come in my pants in Professor Levy's history lecture. She laughed and said she'd once prayed to Brain-God that she could stay a virgin till she was thirteen. Daft, she knew, but she wanted to feel that she was unique, as all thirteen-year-olds do, I suppose. You know, we even touched in the ancient ways, letting our lips, which we hadn't sterilised, moisten each other and nestle in together like baby hamsters. It was the most romantic time I've ever experienced.

I orgasmed several times, and she said she'd never come so often in one sex-spell, Then the moment was broken by her great-grandfather's return. "Hey, you kids," he said, "Time to get back to thinking." He looked much refreshed and I suppose I must have appeared totally exhausted. I had to make quite a cerebral effort to pull myself together, but I was excited by the new discovery Jim said he'd made about VP Johnson. He'd promised to think it across to me as soon as he got back from his break.

But, of course, he never got the chance to tell me what that discovery was. There was a loud whirring of the entry-bell and, before we had a chance to know what was occurring, four burly Thought Police marched into the study where we were sitting. Without a by your leave the officer in charge thought Jim Barrackson his rights and two of his subordinates marched him off to the arresto-centre. I was astonished by this turn of events, but Eva was remarkably calm. She bade me a hurried farewell and ushered me out of the flatlet. I tried to offer what help I could, but in reality I was grateful that the Thinkoes didn't seem to regard me as implicated in whatever offence Jim was being charged with.

For the next few days I tried telescreening Eva to discover what was going on, but there was never any response. Then, on the third day I heard on Thinkovision that a senior TrainerCorp line manager had been arrested for Coke abuse and illicit distilling of McBud. I knew that Jim would be lucky to get away with less than a ten-stretch for such serious felonies, and I tried every means to communicate with Eva, mainly to offer her my sympathies for what her great-grandfather was undergoing. She never replied, however, and it wasn't till about three weeks later that I finally heard what had happened to her. Clearly she loved Jim intensely, as one would expect, of course, but I was still shocked that she decided she could not go on without him. A mental picture of her was broadcast on Thinkovision: she was floating on her back in the lily pond at the end of Jim's communal garden, looking for all the world like a painting of Lizzie Siddons I once saw. I'm not sure what the primitive painter meant to portray – perhaps it was The Lady of Charlotte, or Hamlet's sister Ophelia in the old myth – but the resemblance was astounding. Her long tresses of bright red hair were splayed out like a burning bush on the limpid water of the still pond where she had bottomed herself. She had on the same simple white shift that she'd been wearing when I met her for the second time and our lips bruised like petals as we mutuo-orgasmed. Her face was pellucidly transformed to a sleep-mask of the rarest beauty. Her tiny breasts were gentle hillocks on the sweeping landscape of her smooth young body. I tell you, I intra-sexed on the spot.

The following year President Johnson was arraigned for tax invasion, and it was then that the business of the stain on his suit started to emerge. Because an offence against the tax laws is so serious, it was no surprise that his whole flat and all his possessions were DNA'd. It was never indisputably proved, but suggestions were rife for months that there were traces of grey matter on Johnson's best charcoal suit. Scientists argued hither and thither whether the traces were compatible with President Brian's cerebral fiber tracts, which led a lot of people to question once more exactly what had happened to the big brain. As I say though, nothing was ever proved.

And all of that took place thirty odd years ago. But I'd like to set down this: there was a brain death, certainly, but what are we meant to believe? That people die, and should stay dead? Or that one day they will rise again, freed from their frozen tombs to think and to imagine? It's a problem, as I say. But it's not the only problem. To tell the truth, I miss Eva more than I can say. Miriam's a good womanwife, but naturally we don't kiss. I feel at two with her most of the time, which is as it should be, but that brief time when I felt so at one with a woman haunts me still. It's as if I've been mutilated somehow and I've lost a vital part of myself. But then again, as I think I quoted already, 'so it goes.'

IN THE COUNTRY OF THE DEAF

"There is loss, and there is disease, and there is injury," Dr Jenkins said in his stentorian voice. The four interns trailing after him paused dutifully and looked down at their feet waiting for him to continue after his dramatic pause. "But there are only very occasional examples of self-mutilation that are not due to one of these prerequisites."

The ward round at St Thomas Hospital was nearly over and the last patient to be seen had been a young man who had attempted to cut off his own ear with a kitchen knife. Sara Kennedy, the youngest of the student doctors following the great consultant, had been shocked to hear this, but she thought it now even more shocking that Dr Jenkins could use the poor man's condition as a starting point for a pedantic treatise on self-damage. As the party had drawn to a halt at the bedside of the pale eighteen year old, the ward sister had handed Jenkins a chart, which he had looked at only cursorily. He smirked at the patient but said nothing to him. Instead, he turned to Sara and her three colleagues and sighed. "The erysipelas epidemic of 1089, for instance, was a particularly virulent streptococcus which attacked the ears, faces and necks of the good citizenry of Ghent. The effects of this virus caused these poor people to attack their own ear lobes with notched knives – the serrations being suited to a sawing motion – and to cut off one, or sometimes both, of their ears. Some of these souls survived in their disfigured ..." He paused to suppress a smile, "but you have to say *streamlined* state. Others died of bleeding, or shock, or various haematological toxins."

Sara could tell that this lesson from history was less to do with ENT than a need her mentor must have felt to air his encyclopaedic knowledge. It was a piece of showmanship, but in an odd way she found it interesting too. She had always known that history held important lessons, but it had been something she had been forced to recognise with far greater urgency since her father's sad death a few months before. Indeed, it had been looking through his notebooks and charts that had sparked a missionary zeal to find out more about her family's genealogy. Perhaps Dr Martin Jenkins saw something of that bright eagerness in her face. Perhaps he simply had a predilection for fresh young student doctors, and had never been with a black woman before. Either way, Sara fancied he was talking to her more directly than to the others, as he gave his sardonic speech.

As soon as they had left the young man's bedside and were out in the corridor once more, she decided to risk a question. "So what do you think of the famous case of Van Gogh, Dr Jenkins?"

He looked at her more intently. "I go by Mr Jenkins these days," he said, "But a good question, Miss..."

"Kennedy."

"Exactly. As you no doubt have read, Van Gogh suffered from a maddening, agonising streptococcal itch. He must have felt like a cat you see lashing out at itself. They'll make their own ears bleed in an attempt to dislodge or kill an invading flea, won't they? Our Dutch friend must have lashed out in the same manner. He actually lopped off part of his own concha, leaving an exposed tragus, antitragus and scaphal furrow."

Sara smiled, though the other student doctors were still studying their own footwear with pained intensity. "Lots of people still believe other accounts though, don't they?" she said. "Haven't critics argued that it was his inordinate consumption of absinthe that caused him to have some form of hallucinatory fit?"

Dr Jenkins furrowed his dark brows. "You can argue it was drink; you can also argue it was self-loathing, caused by his sexual encounters with prostitutes, that caused the mutilatory act, but I prefer the scientific explanation."

Sara was even more certain that he was flirting with her. There was something self-conscious about the way that he stroked his greying temple before speaking again, and once more his words were directed at her, rather than the group. "Of course we can compare such an act to

93

the self-mutilation of certain slaves in America in the nineteenth century," he added.

The brave consultant was a man of striking appearance, tall, suave, and even handsomer than the reports Sara had already heard from the star struck young female doctors and nurses at St Thomas. He was younger than she'd imagined too. Frankly, she considered, he was an absolute dish, but this last remark disturbed her. Nevertheless, she was flattered when he chose to sit down beside her in the canteen a couple of days later, and her instinct was initially to dismiss his racial slur as over-sensitivity on her own part. She was staring into space as he approached her table and she was more than a little surprised when he asked if he could join her.

She smiled and he immediately began talking. "How are you settling in at St Thomas? he asked.

"Fine, but I expect the six months will fly. I hope not, because it's an excellent hospital."

"Particularly noted for its Ear, Nose and Throat Department too, I believe."

She smiled, hoping that this self-regard was intended in part as self-mockery.

"Where would you like to end up working," he said. "Do you mind if I ask you where you're from, by the way? I hope you don't think I'm being impertinent."

Sara had thought that the only legitimate topic of conversation would be medical matters, but she found his urbane bedside manner somewhat seductive. She suddenly didn't mind talking about herself. "That's a very pertinent question, as it happens," she said. "I'm from Bristol. I'm first generation English. My father came to England from Jamaica in the early sixties. My great-great grandfather was actually white, you know." She laughed. "But that was some time ago, of course."

"Really?" he said. This time there was no irony in his expression.

"Really," she said. "My father died not long ago, but he spent his last few years researching into our family history. It's quite a piece of work actually, especially when you consider that our name is such a common one, and that records didn't use to be anything like as efficiently kept back in Jamaica as they probably are here."

Jenkins seemed genuinely interested.

"Dad managed to construct a family tree way back to the eighteenth century, which I think is quite a feat."

He agreed. "That's probably more than many a family could do," he said. "Even one that's spent all its existence in one small part of Britain."

"It's possible that a branch of my family settled in Louisiana even before it became part of the United States." Sara's voice became more animated as she pursued the theme that had recently become so important to her. "But before that," she added, "Our ancestors were pirates. Can you believe that Dr Jenkins? And before that even, they were respectable traders."

"How did you find out all this?" he asked. "Oh, I'm sorry, by the way, I know you as Miss Kennedy. You'll have to remind me of your first name, forgive me."

"I'm called Sara," she said.

"Of course," he said quickly, "Stupid of me to temporarily disremember that. But with a name like Kennedy should I guess that you have Irish ancestry too then?

She smiled. "I know that would be a logical thing to think, but surprisingly no, nothing like that has turned up. Not everyone is as they seem. Apparently one of my ancestors changed his name to Kennedy because he liked the sound of it. That sort of thing happened a lot with immigrants to America, didn't it? I guess it can happen anywhere though."

"I must say," Jenkins sighed. "I've never taken much interest in my own family's origins, but I'm fascinated to hear that you're from sea-going stock. One thing I have heard from my own family legends is that I'm supposed to be descended from naval men."

"I wonder if they were respectable captains and admirals," Sara said, "Or pirates and adventurers, like my forefathers. But they say, don't they, that everyone on earth is only six times removed from anyone else on the planet. Perhaps we are related." She laughed loudly at her own joke, but his face stayed serious. "Well, I know this isn't very interesting for you," she went on, "But it was my late father's passion, and I kind of think I owe it to him to continue the quest as far as I can, that's all."

"I hope your work here allows you time for such passion," he said.

Sara was uncertain whether she should take this remark as a rebuke, for he stressed the word *passion* and all of a sudden she felt a twinge of embarrassment that was nothing to do with what she'd said about her personal preoccupation. She tried to joke her way out of it. "I'm not saying I'm an Alex Haley fan or anything. Anyway, we can't find any West African connections. I just try to use my spare time productively."

"You are a very beautiful woman," he said, right out of the blue, "But you'll have to excuse me, I have to get back to my office. Perhaps we could have lunch together again?"

Sara gave a half-smile. "I'm sorry if I've been boring you."

He looked at her broad ebony face for a moment before speaking. "I'll have none of that. I'd like to hear more. Could we make it dinner instead of lunch?"

She wanted to say it wouldn't be right, as much because of the professional situation as anything else, but he would not let her speak. "We'll arrange something for the weekend," he said. "I'll speak to you tomorrow."

"Aren't you married, Dr Jenkins?"

"Please call me Martin. While we're not on the ward anyway. Yes I am, but my wife doesn't understand me". He gave a wry grin. "She works in London most of the time. That's the thing with two professional people like us working in similar fields, you have to go where the work is."

Sara said nothing more, but the following day, at the end of another ward round, Martin took her by the arm and said a few words in her ear. Almost without knowing it she had agreed to an assignation. They were to meet at The Duke, a mock-Victorian pub not far from her city centre flat, at six thirty the next evening.

She was uncertain whether Martin had been simply suggesting a late afternoon drink between workfellows, or whether he meant a proper date, beginning with an early aperitif. She decided to pick out a pair of khaki shorts, though the weather didn't really warrant them, and a tight purple top. To confirm that she only intended a platonic relationship she tucked a slim leather case under her arm. She looked at herself in the hall mirror and was pleased by her appearance. The effect was a strange blend of casual and business-like. She draped a tan leather jacket over her shoulders, then at the last moment she took out her gold studs and replaced them with a pair of large bright red plastic earrings. They were garish, but they were fun.

The Duke was one of those pubs that had been refurbished in the nineteen eighties with a central bar and plenty of good wood, with some discreet seating for early evening couples but a lot of floor space for the younger crowd who stand about in huddles and take their drinking more seriously. Sara ordered a Jim Beam on ice and sat down in a corner to wait for her date. When Martin walked in he looked a little more flustered than normal. "I had a tonsillectomy that was trickier than usual," he said. "I'm sorry I'm a bit late." He looked down at the leather case on Sara's lap. "What have you got there, sheet music? Am I holding you up from orchestra practice or something?"

Sara thought perhaps his impudence was intended to come across as boyish good humour. "I just thought you might be interested in what we were talking about the other day," she said. "Would you like a look? It's a family tree that my father drew up."

He unfolded the A3 sheet that she offered him and scrutinised the tiny writing. "There's an awful lot of people," he said.

"And a fair number of dead ends, sadly," she said. "But you can only do so much. Do you think computer records will mean that in five hundred years everyone will know everything they ever need to know

97

about where they came from?"

"I'm not sure if people in five hundred years will care very much," he answered. "And they'll probably have the same difficulty deciphering our primitive computer languages that we do today translating dead languages."

Sara thought about this, "Yes, you may be right," she said. "But this is what I really wanted to show you..." She took out a document in a transparent plastic folder. It was a photocopy of what looked like an ancient legal transcript.

"What's this? He said.

"It's the proceedings from a parliamentary sub-committee to investigate admiralty issues. Look at the date – 1738."

"Is this from Hansard?" he said in some surprise.

"No, it's from a library in Baton Rouge."

Martin studied the document closely. He clearly had trouble reading it, however, perhaps because he found it hard to follow the syntax and archaic vocabulary.

"I'll paraphrase it for you," Sara said. She took the document off him and began to scan through it, although it seemed like she was reading from memory, not from the page, when she began to speak. "It's Captain Robert Jenkins' deposition to the Admiralty petitioning for action to be taken against the Spanish for the ritual humiliation he suffered at their hands." She looked up. "Did you ever hear of the War of Jenkins' Ear? I was looking at this yesterday and I had the weirdest idea. Perhaps Captain Robert Jenkins Was one of your naval ancestors!"

Martin's eyes widened. "Well, I doubt that. He's probably too famous for my modest line. I do recall something about a stupidly named war though. I had to study eighteenth century history when I was at school. A very long time ago, you understand."

"Well listen to this," Sara said. "Wouldn't it be amazing if he was your great-great-great grandfather or something?" She began reading from the manuscript. "The brigands bound and gagged me in front of my own men, then a man called Manuel Lopes, whose soul I hope will rot forever..." She paused and let her eyes rove over the page. "Anyway, he goes on about that for a while, but the gist of it is this: a Spanish guy steps forward and bites off his ear, then spits it out into the ocean. Then there's some stuff about losses sustained in terms of cargo. Isn't it kind of weird to imagine the scene though? I guess he spat the ear overboard to prevent the captain retrieving it and sewing it back on. But they wouldn't have had the technology to do that back then, I suppose, would they?"

"He could have sewn it back on, even then," Martin said. "But there wouldn't have been much point, apart from some cosmetic advantage. But it sounds like Captain Jenkins wasn't in much of a position to requisition urgent surgery, if he was a prisoner of the Spanish."

She looked at him with soft brown eyes afire with simultaneous curiosity and mirth. "Are you making fun of me, Martin?"

"Not at all. He sounds lucky to have escaped with his life, that's what I meant." Then, sensing a certain scepticism, he spoke again. "I was offering a serious prognosis, with historical accuracy in mind."

"My foot!"

"I'm Ear, Nose and Throat, not feet," he said.

She took a sip of her Jim Beam and put away the document. "So," she continued, "I know you've never thought about it, but if the captain was an ancestor of yours, and if you'd ever wondered how he lost an ear you would probably have thought it was in some manly sword fight. I can now report to you that in fact he was treated like an early Evander Holyfield. In a less than fair fight, it has to be said. It's an animalistic thing to do though, isn't it?"

"Well, it isn't very friendly."

"No, I'm being literal. I mean, it's the sort of attack that an animal perpetrates on one of its own species, don't you think? Like when cats and dogs fight each other, they tend to go for the ears, right?"

"I've never thought about it. But it reminds me of that Tarantino movie *Reservoir Dogs*. Michael Madsen chops off the policeman's ear, doesn't he? That's the same kind of thing – humiliation – though he does go on to kill him of course. Did you ever see that film?"

Sara replied that she had. What struck her about the scene was the way the violence was conducted like a ballet. "Strange soundtrack too. *Stuck in the Middle with You*, wasn't it? I used to love that song."

"I'm into jazz and blues myself." There was too long a lull. But anyway, what did the Admiralty think of Captain Jenkins' deposition?"

"Well, initially they weren't too impressed apparently. The attack had actually happened four years before. It's a bit like someone with whiplash figuring they can make something out of it much later on. Maybe someone told him he could sue the government over it, some eighteenth century Lawyers R Us outfit."

"You have done your research on this, haven't you?" he said.

"I'm only carrying on what my father started. Listen, I'm sorry if I got it wrong and you're not interested in any of this..."

"No, please, it's fascinating," he said quickly. "But I suppose I always thought that history was about people like kings and queens. In our case, that is. Or presidents maybe. Not people I might actually be related to, I mean."

"History's about people, Martin," Sara said seriously. "We're all related to each other in some way, simply be being people."

Martin shrugged.

Sara decided to bring up what had been troubling her. "What did you mean when you were talking about Van Gogh and you mentioned slaves mutilating themselves, Martin? Wasn't that a massive generalisation? What evidence have you got for saying that?"

"What? Oh, the blacks in Alabama and Georgia, you mean?" He was embarrassed, Sara felt, by his own bluntness, but he pressed on blithely. "It's all in the literature. There's a tradition for certain African women to cut off their daughter's clitoris, you must know that. It's like Chinese women binding their daughter's feet and tribes piercing their own bodies. Women seem to have felt the need to abuse themselves and each other over the centuries."

"And men don't practise self-abuse?"

"That's different." He smiled broadly. "You're just debating with me now."

"Okay," she replied, "but you seem so smug as you say that, like it's a fault in the line. Surely it's the tyranny of men that causes women to punish their bodies."

"So what are you saying? That men like me make women wear facial jewellery? Who is it that goes round forcing girls to pierce their navels and their lips? And their eyebrows and goodness knows what else?"

Sara happened to be fingering one of her big red earrings as he spoke. She let her hand fall to her laps as she saw him smirk. "There's a difference between making your body beautiful and desecrating it though. Yes, I have pierced ears, and I'll be frank with you, I have a pierced nipple too."

"I'd like to see that," Martin said. "For research purposes, you understand. Is there anything else you'd like to reveal?"

Sara took a large gulp of her drink. She looked like she'd had enough.

"I'm only joking," Martin said quickly. "Sorry, that was adolescent of me."

"It was," Sara said sharply, "I thought you'd be more mature than that."

"Actually, I deplore the damage that people do to their bodies. It's part of the Hippocratic territory to do so, don't you think? But I still find certain things exciting. I'm a man after all."

Sara regained some of her composure. "Well, I have a tattoo," she said, sounding demure.

"Where? No, let me guess. On your shoulder?"

"No, that's far too conventional," Sara laughed. "On my derriere, if you insist on asking."

"And what does it say? 'I love Dad', perhaps?"

Sara made an important decision at this point. It was one that would change her future, at least in terms of her immediate career. She took a breath. "It's not like a sailor's tattoo, Martin," she said. "It's a lot more tasteful than that. It's quite beautiful, in fact." She imagined a crudely carved rose on her left buttock, with large deep red petals and a gross thick green stem. "But if you want to appreciate the artistry at first hand, so to speak, you'll have to get me another drink."

Martin nodded at her glass. "Same again? If you like, we'll have a couple more here, then we could go back to my flat and listen to some music. I imagine you're a fan of the blues too, if you've got connections to Louisiana, as you say."

When he returned from the bar Sara let him run through a list of his favourite blues artists. She even let him recite the lyrics of a Howlin' Wolf number – '*I asked for water, she brought me gasoline*'. Then talk turned to more neutral matters, such as Sara's training experience and Martin's rise to the dizzy heights of his current status at St Thomas. She let him pursue this topic for a while, then she interrupted with a bolder question. "And do you try to sleep with all your female interns, Martin?"

He gave a nervous laugh. "Not all of them. You're a very attractive girl, Sara."

"But a man in your position must get plenty of opportunities," she goaded.

"Women certainly like power," he said calmly. "But I'm not a gynaecologist. I believe that would have made me more attractive to some girls."

"If you assume that all a girl wants is a certain degree of vaginal expertise, I suppose."

He shrugged, but still showed no sign of embarrassment. "I take it you are the sort of girl who'd prefer flowers and fine and fancy phrases?"

"I do like flowers actually." She smiled to herself. "I've already told you about my rose tattoo. But I can do without stupid flattery and all the old lines that men give out like fliers."

"But it's all a bit of a game, isn't it," Martin said. "I say you are beautiful, you give a coy smile and play with your hair."

Sara's eyes widened. "I don't have that sort of hair, do I? Are you trying to say that all your students are bimbos?"

"Not all, obviously. Some of them are intelligent, modern young women with striking personalities."

"And pierced nipples?"

"And pierced nipples."

She gave a throaty laugh. "Okay then, Mr Top Consultant, that's a convincing enough line. Let's go back to your place and listen to your seduction tapes."

***

On the cab journey Martin ran a hand through the tight curls of his companion's think black hair. "It's like a bush," he said.

"You'd better be careful you don't get your hand caught in it then."

Martin chuckled. "I really think I'm taking to you," he said.

Sara did not feel the need to make the regulation remarks about Martin's flat being nice. She took in the regency striped wallpaper and the hardback books on the shelves in a single glance, then turned and peeled off her leather jacket, carelessly flinging it on a chair before slumping onto a chesterfield. Martin asked her what she wanted to drink as he poured himself a sizeable Glenmorangie.

"I'll have a small sherry, if you have one," she said.

"No, is that really what you want?"

"What I really want is a cranapple juice, but I bet you don't have that, do you? The sherry was a joke, by the way. I could use a beer actually. Hey, where's your refrigerator anyway?" She looked round the living room for a huge white wardrobe, as if she were in an American sitcom.

"I keep it in the kitchen," Martin said. "Silly, I know, but I suppose I'm just an old fashioned guy at heart."

"No, you're kidding me?"

He quickly stepped into the small kitchen and located a can of Heineken. As he handed it over he sat down beside her and kicked off his Hush Puppies. "Old fashioned in some ways anyway. Not too much, I hope. How much would you appreciate?"

She gave a false smile and flicked open the tab of her can. "You've got to find the right level yourself, Martin. Isn't that the fun part?"

For some reason a blush started to form on Martin's cheek and he put his cool whisky tumbler to his check to forestall it.

"It's all fun, Sara," he said. "You know, I really like being with you."

She leaned over and brushed his cheek with her lips. Then she nuzzled his ear lobe. He moaned slowly at the damp sensation as her tongue flicked around his ear. But at the same time he wanted to seize control himself. He tried to turn her face towards him but suddenly she bit hard at his ear and a stabbing pain jolted him away.

"Jesus!" he cried, "Wow! That hurt."

She sat back up and raised her Heineken to her reddened lips. She said nothing and he resolved to start again. He placed one hand on her knee and she didn't move, but neither did she register any emotion. She was staring ahead at a Miro reproduction on the wall behind the television.

He followed her line of vision. "What are you thinking?" he said. "It's by Miro, if that's what you were wondering."

I know," she said. She put down her drink on the glass coffee table before them and unbuttoned the top button of her blouse. He quickly downed the rest of his whisky, coughing as he swallowed a splinter of ice, and moved towards her meaningfully.

"Slowly," she said, and she kissed him on the lips. As he was about to respond, she ducked her head into his shoulder again. Once more he felt her teeth nipping at the lobe of his right ear. He relaxed and manoeuvred his hand underneath the belt of her shorts so he could pull out her blouse. At that point she sank her teeth fully into his ear lobe again. He yelped and pushed her off with one hand. He instinctively clapped his other hand to the side of his head and his face burned as he felt a warm bead of blood on his finger.

"The sins of the fathers, Martin," she said. He was wearing a complacent smile. "Even you must know that's true."

"What?"

"Nothing. Say, what's black and white and red all over?"

He scowled, uninterested in stupid schoolyard riddles as he continued dabbing at his ear.

"Me, and you, and you ear, Martin!" she said gleefully.

"I don't understand," he said. He saw a look of playful disappointment cross her face. "I don't mean your stupid joke. I mean, why do you want to inflict pain? Did I hurt you in some way?"

"Not especially. I'm only playing, Martin. Playing with your arrogance and your ignorance. It's just a little history lesson, is all. But don't worry, you won't learn from it. You'll tell your friends you had an encounter with a crazy black girl and you kicked her out. That's all. She drained her can and stood up. "But hey, thanks for the drink."

He got up and gave her a hurt, serious look.

"I'll get a cab out on the street," she said. "You can put your blues records on after I've gone. Oh, and Dr Jenkins, don't look like that, it's not as personal as you're making it out. Any more than it ever was. For every black woman who got raped, or beaten, or circumcised. And by the way, I don't do tattoos, or nipple rings. Or big brass rings through my nose, for that matter. If you're serious about your personal researches, I'd recommend you try the *literature*, as you put it. You could start with the *Asiento De Negros*. It's a record of assent from the days of the slave trade. But it may not be your sort of history, Martin... It's not about kings and queens, it's about real people. Oh, and if you're thinking of what you might do to get back at me for this in work, don't bother. I won't be going back to St Thomas."

A VERY PRIVATE GARDEN

Sir Clifford took a sip of his Amontillado and picked up the leather bound Baudelaire that lay on the davenport beside him. "Shall I read to you?" he said to his wife. She nodded, but without much sign of interest. She was running her long tapered fingers through the rich coils of hair thrown back over her shoulders. Clifford smiled, then began to read in a rich, polished drawl: "For hands she hath none, nor eyes, nor feet, golden treasure of hair' – unlike you, darling," he added.

"Oh, read it in French," she said impatiently, "You know I love your accent."

He raised his head from the book and she caught his rather prominent pale eyes giving her a quizzical look, then he continued in the exquisite tones of the original language.

Connie was thinking about other tones, however. She was recalling the broad Nottinghamshire vowels of her afternoon lover. "Am't bods in't coop?" he'd said. And she'd wondered if he was making fun of her, for she knew she couldn't help wrinkling up her petite nose when he used his quaint dialect. "Why, I believe I could bring thee off just with speaking to thee," he'd said the previous time. "Ah, Lady Cunnie, tha's a reet little shag, and no mistake, but am I to show thee position number forty one now? I'll be ready agin in next to no time."

At the same time that Clifford's antique French participles were flowing through the cortices of her brain, she felt the power of Mellors' manhood pulsing through her unresisting body like a mountain brook coursing through a deep ravine. Or perhaps less a brook than a rocky white avalanche tumbling down a crevasse.

Sir Clifford stopped reading and examined his wife's expression. Her eyes were closed and her facial muscles tensed, almost as if she was in pain. She was beautiful, of course, her slightly flared nostrils and the flow of her deep auburn mane giving her the air of a proud but frightened mare.

There was a soft rap at the panelled door. "Ah, Mrs Bolton," Sir Clifford said. "Tea."

Mrs Bolton was a large woman with thick arms and fleshy calves that swelled from the floral dress she wore beneath her starched pinafore. She sighed as she laid the tea things down on a highly polished walnut occasional table. "Would you like me to pour?" she said.

Sir Clifford gestured her away. "We'll let it stew awhile," he declared. "Has Mellors delivered the pheasants yet?"

Mrs Bolton shook her head with the lazy irony of her class. "I'm sure he'll be up before long, Sir Clifford. He comes quite regular, you know."

"Quite so. Well, that will be all for now, Mrs B."

She withdrew softly, pulling the door to behind her with the gravity of a relative saddened by the imminent loss of a loved one.

"That woman has the impudence of the devil," Connie said suddenly. She pulled herself up in her winged armchair and reached for the teapot.

"Let me do that," her husband insisted. "Just a teaspoon of milk, as always, my dear?"

She tried to smile, but her lips seemed locked in a rictus of domestic paralysis as she watched her husband leak a few drops of the pale liquid into her cup.

***

Oliver Mellors, meanwhile, was mashing a dark brew of Horniman's finest blended Ceylon tea in his hut in High Park Wood. "A reet shag indeed," he muttered out loud, though of course there was no one to hear him, or the snorting laugh which followed his utterance. "I should quit this damn place and go to America. Try a new air."

It was towards evening when he had been approaching his hut. It was that time when the summer light began to soften the harsh daylight greens and sepias of the hedgerows and woody ferns, modulating those shades to the hues of a Monet lily pond. He had been thinking about his recent tryst with the lady from Wragby Hall as he stepped through the brakes and brambles to reach the narrow path to his private abode. Then he had been taken short. He had had to stop by a bramble bush to lower his corduroys and ease his bowels, which he did slowly and without discomfort, despite having to balance on his haunches. His expressionless stare straight ahead as he crouched a few inches above the musky damp grass was that of a house cat being watched from an upstairs window in this most private of acts. But there was no living creature to attend to the performance. The birds were still abroad, swooping and careening above the topmost branches of the oaks, and the more secret denizens of the wood were still ensconced within their sets and dens, waiting for some exact crepuscular signal to summon their emergence. He rather wished he could have had something other than broad leafed grass to cleanse himself, but he was glad too that he had left the limp paper novel he was reading back in the hut, for he might have been tempted to rip out a page or two. In such a case, what would a man do? Tear out the title page, and perhaps stain the author's name? Perhaps use the verso, in order only to despoil the publisher's details? Would it matter if you used the opening pages of the story, when you had already read the first few chapters and knew what was happening?

Now, back in the hut, he picked up the novel, a flimsy tale of romance and despair, and riffled through the yellowing pages. It was only another man's ideas, or another man's lies and fantasies. Life was for living, not for reading about. Still, he determined, he would probably finish his reading before he broke the spine and tore out the pages, prior to forcing them over the nail on the back of the privy door.

By the light of his oil lamp he let the words pass before his eyes. Words, words, words, Hamlet said, but what did Hamlet know? There were other words, or rather, deeper expressions, that told of a man's true narrative. Deep within his bowels Mellors felt his own story unfolding: it was a paean to manly love with a dashing fair haired colonel; it was a saga of rapine mutual destruction with a Tevershall lass called Bertha; it was an incipit of floral beatitudes with the heavy limbed, ruddy complexioned Connie. How strange that Lady Chatterley bore the same Christian name as his own daughter! And stranger, how the fruit of his peasant loins was a far more delicate and fragile bloom than the rough petalled aristocratic Scot! Young Connie was, of course, her mother's daughter too. There was something bold and brazen about the girl's oval eyes and her gap-toothed letterbox of a smile that recalled Bertha's insolent insouciance. But still, Connie's other features were small and pale, only faintly darkened by the chiaroscuro shadow of the woman she would one day become.

Mellors thought about Millie, the braw teenage colleen he had met at Blackrock two decades before, and imagined how her face might have transmuted from its soft, round newness to the harder lines of womanhood. Her lilting Hibernian tones would have sharpened, whetted by bitterness, to the washer woman cackle of a Dublin drab by now, no doubt. Her life's narrative would be a discordant contrapuntal motif to the sentimentalising airs of her native land.

But if Mellors were to tell his own story, what notes would be heard? Would they be the naive crotchets of his native, once rejected, now once again adopted Midlands dialect? Or would they be the low, slow breves of a man once commissioned to the ranks of authority; the more languorous diphthongs of a class that did little but talk? The lieutenant turned gamekeeper took a long draft of his Horniman's from his still hot enamel mug and then he let his lips purse into a narrow and bitter smile once again.

∗∗∗

Sir Clifford, meanwhile, was setting down the dregs of his tea. His wife had apparently dozed off, but he did not mind. He saw that he could quietly slip away and spend some time in the library. He was looking forward to continuing with his latest offering to the literary world. It was to be a short tale for the illustrated papers about a man who had been maimed in the Great War, only to find on his return to his village that he could now connect, as a whole being, with the hum and thrum of industrial life. The sex thing was, of course, of little importance. The urgent beat of the body was as nought compared to the susurration of the mind and the soul. What mattered in the age of the bar room was art, not the heart; the artisan, not the courtesan. In the age of the salon men and women had tried to meld form and experience through the aesthetics of pulchritude and pornography. Renoir had painted with his penis, or so Michaelis, the jaded terrorist, had claimed after dinner at Wragby Hall. But Sir Clifford knew that Picasso and Ernst were dabblers and dreamers. Only by the wordsmith's artifice could the true shape, the ineffable *nebeneinander* of things, be expressed with veracity. And it was with this article of faith firmly in mind that he drew up his wheelchair to the desk, took out a blacklead from the drawer, and opened a slim exercise book to begin his story.

As her husband sat at his desk struggling to capture the precise odour of a night time garden – the lavender, the chrysanthemums, the reek of sage and mint – as an introductory setting for his protagonist, the maimed Guardsman, Connie stirred in her chair in the living room. She had not been asleep for she had closed her eyes to think. Her mind was on flowers too. She was recalling the absolute tenderness with which her afternoon lover had threaded forget-me-nots into her dark bush of pubic hair. His hands had plied the stems with a craftsman's care. His long, surprisingly slender fingers had looked almost like a girl's as he lovingly plaited the green and the brown in a soft trailing trellis. She was reminded of a painting she had seen in the National Gallery the previous Spring, where a girl of fifteen or so was portrayed sitting in a field of poppies, her mind engrossed by the grass, her countenance still as the air, her silence more powerful even than that ghastly oval shriek of the girl in the painting by that fearful Norwegian maniac, Edvard Munch. The girl in the painting might have almost been the same girl that Wordsworth had heard singling as she reaped in the Highlands a century earlier.

Connie Chatterley was brought back to that afternoon's bucolic charms by a shocking memory of Mellors' words as he surveyed his artwork: "Tha's gut a fancy little fanny nah," he'd said. "Hasn't ter?"

"You make me look I'm growing," she'd rejoined. "Like I'm part of the natural world."

"Persephone personified, you might say." The sudden jarring transition from the twang of his native tongue to the elegance of this witty homophone delighted and bemused her in equal measure.

"I feel like I'm Echo to your Narcissus," she murmured.

"There's no need to patronise me, your ladyship," Mellors replied sharply. "I may not have a classical education, but I know what a man may do and what a man may dream."

"But I did not mean to offend you," she said quickly. "I thought you must have knowledge of the myths when you spoke of Persephone just then. You are a man of many parts, I believe."

"All men must play many parts in their short stay on this stage, Cunnie."

"Why, what do you mean by that? Are you saying you're merely acting out a role when we're together like this?"

"I mean, your ladyship, that a man may be master and servant at one and the same time. And more than that. He mun be bairn and father, ally and enemy, dolt and wise man, all at t' identical stroke of t' clock."

I think you are making fun of me now."

"And whyfore dost that reckon to that nah, Mrs?"

At this moment she moved his hand, which was resting on her mons veneris. She pushed it to one side so that she could pinch together the petals of a single forget-me-not. "There, I have crushed your masterwork," she said triumphantly. "If you mock me, I will mar you."

That sounds like Shakespeare tha's quoting me," Mellors said gruffly.

"It's not Shakespeare," Connie laughed. "That was me. Can a woman not say poetic things? Why should we not have a voice too?"

"I suppose tha's reet. But there's another poet, I don't think it was Shakespeare, who spoke for most men in these matters. 'For God's sake,

112

hold thy tongue and let me love,' he said. And that's what I think tha should do now." He put his hand back where it had lain a moment before and at the same time kissed her roughly on the lips.

***

Mrs Bolton sat down in her wicker chair at one end of the long basement kitchen and picked up her knitting. Pushing herself deeper into the pile of flowered cushions on the chair she began to sing, in her tuneless contralto voice, a melody from a contemporary popular show. Molly, the kitchen maid, looked up from the table where she was peeling vegetables for dinner and grimaced. "Tha sounds like a kitten drownding, Mrs B," she said. "Has ter gi' it a rest, for t' sake o' us all?"

"That's enough of your cheek, madam," Mrs Bolton replied, but without severity. "I'm allowed to hear my own voice, aren't I?"

"Well, couldn't tha at least choose something a mickle more heartening, if tha's a need to air thee tonsils? That's a reet dirge for a Monday afternoon, or leastways tha' makes it seem so."

"It's a sad little ditty about a young man who's lost his love, my girl. What do you expect, a guardsman's march?" Despite her protestations, however, Mrs Bolton was fond of the blunt good humour of the kitchen maid, and was content enough on this occasion to stop singing and concentrate on the garment she was knitting for her young nephew's birthday.

It was not long before Molly spoke again. "The maister's a fine man, in his own manner, isn't he, Mrs B?" she said slyly.

"Whatever's on your mind now, girl?" Mrs Bolton replied, looking up from a slipstitch with some perturbation in her cheeks. "What on earth makes you say such a thing out of the blue like that?"

"Nuthin."

"Well, you want to make sure no one else hears your nothings. People are like to think they're sweet nothings. Or sour perhaps, which would make it go worse for you, mayhap."

113

"I was just thinking that her ladyship mun pay a little more heed to her master, that's all. What with her hitherings and thitherings all over the park, she's scarce ever at home to bide with Sir Clifford and make his ease, so to speak."

"And what would a lady's comings and goings have to do with one of her scullions, I may ask?" the older woman said quickly. But though her words were harsh, her tone was more inquisitive than admonitory.

"A cat may look at a queen, mayn't she?" Molly said, sounding almost hurt, despite the mildness of Mrs Bolton's tone.

"Ay, but she may not scratch."

"I meant no offence. I just think Mr Clifford has a look about him sometimes. You know, like he's lost his purse and found tuppence."

"Well, he certainly hasn't seen m'lady's tuppence for a while," Mrs Bolton burst out, though she said it to amuse herself rather than directly to Molly.

Molly had heard nonetheless. "Ooh, Mrs B." she tittered. "You are a one!"

Mrs Bolton sighed and looked serious again. "But I fears tha's right about her ladyship and that bold gamekeeper of ourn."

Molly put down her paring knife. She went to speak, then hesitated.

"What's up with thee now?" Mrs Bolton said.

"It's just ... I meantersay... do you ever think that girls has got something missing, mum," she said.

"Aye, a couple or three brain cells, mayhap, Or at least we mun have, working down here in t' dank cold kitchen while them upstairs is lounging about on soft sofas reading books and whatnot."

"Tha knows what I'm trying to say, Mrs B. Like we're not quite complete in oursen."

"I do know, Molly, but look at the other side o' it. Would you seriously want a great dangling bit o' meat and tripes hanging down there? Honestly, I don't know how menfolk walk about sometimes."

Molly giggled. "Do you know, I've never seen a man's thing," she whispered. "Is it a terrible thing to look upon?"

"Tha shouldn't be asking that sort of question, young lady." Mrs Bolton's expression glazed over momentarily. "But it depends on whether it's sleeping, I suppose."

Molly sat down on one of the bentwood chairs by the big old kitchen table. She cupped her chin between chapped hands.

Mrs Bolton spoke again. "If it's awake it can be a monster. If it's not awake it's a pathetic sort of thing. That's all there is to it. Now get on wi' them carrots."

Molly reluctantly picked up a stout knobbly carrot and held it up before her face. Both women burst into giggles, which did not cease until a brass bell tinkled in the wall mounted cabinet above their heads. Mrs Bolton looked up and saw that it was the drawing room bell.

Lady Constance Chatterley had pulled the knob by the fireplace to summon up the housekeeper to remove the tea things. She was suddenly bored and frustrated with the china in front of her, by the dying embers in the hearth, by the heavy slow beat of the ormolu mantel clock.

"Take it all away," she said sharply, as Mrs Bolton appeared in the doorway.

Lady Chatterley wanted a baby. She now knew this with a force that took her aback, like stepping out of doors into an easterly wind. She was empty and aching. She jumped up out of her seat, tutting at the noise Mrs Bolton was making with the crockery, and moved quickly towards the window. It was dusk, and a bat was flitting round an elm tree in the garden before her. Outside, all was gloomy and silent. She tried to pick out familiar objects; the two stone lions at the foot of the terrace, the sundial in the centre of the courtyard, but they had lost shape and texture in the failing light. Everything's asleep, she thought, and nothing can penetrate this stagnant death-in-life.

She loved her home, of course. She loved the contours and

grandeur of Wragby Hall itself, but she loved more the grounds, and in particular her own private garden, which Clifford had allowed her to cultivate according to her own tastes. Here, hypericum and hawthorn hedges acted as stout outer walls to her secret haven. The former, with its dense evergreen leaves and showy, saucer-shaped, bright yellow flowers, was still in bloom, as were some of her favourite flowers. In wide borders she had grown freesias, chrysanthemums, delphiniums, hydrangea, lisianthus, and even a few types of orchid, like cymbidium and oncidium. She loved the audacious colours and the evident struggle between the hardiest and the most delicate of nature's floribunda. Frequently she would relax on a green cast iron bench at one end of this secluded area and smile at the pansies, the fuchsias and the begonias as she looked up from a book. Sometimes, like a young girl again, she would plait buttercups and daisies in a delicate chain before tossing aside such trivialities and returning to her book, or to the house. It was, of course, no longer summer, and autumn's prevarications before the onset of winter's dead hand meant that her sojourns in the garden were ever more brief. Still, she thought, as she looked out of the drawing room window, it is not yet that cold, and dinner is not for another hour or so. She determined to go out to the garden and take in the early evening pungency of her flower borders and the dew softened grass of the lawn.

She slipped on a long beige cardigan from the cupboard in the rear hallway and exited the house via the back door. The air was scented already with imminent rain as she made her way round the west wing of the house to the picket gate entrance to her garden. There was still a blue band of daylight above the hedging but the heavy dark cloud which had formed meant that nightfall would be sudden and the last rays of warmth would disappear without notice. She pulled the cardigan about her and walked slowly towards a patch of blood red phlox on the far side of the little garden. Here too there were bright yellow cockscomb and deep purple celosia erupting proudly like rockets or roman candles. She felt a surge of longing again, but for what she was unsure. A wind began a low moan in the distance.

How long she had been standing in her private sanctuary she was not clear, but she was awoken from her reverie by the sound of boots crunching on the gravel path a few yards to the left and outside the garden.

"Hello," she called out. "Is that you, Mrs Bolton?"

""Aha," came back a man's deeper tones. "Dost think tha housekeeper has a man's footfall then?"

It was Mellors. She skipped across to the picket gate and confronted him in the shade of a yew tree just outside the little garden. A pair of scrawny pheasants hung limply from his hand. He pushed back, but declined to doff, his cap. "Tha'll catch thy death out here, Mrs," he said.

"I was just about to go back inside," Connie replied, still looking down at the dead birds he was clutching by the gizzards.

"I shan't accompany yer, It wouldn't be seemly. I've to go to t' back door to gi' Mrs Bolton these. Yer'll dine well tonight, I shouldn't doubt."

He made to move away but Connie reached out a hand. "Stay," she said. "Just for a moment. I feel so empty tonight."

"Happen these'll fill thee," he said.

"I don't mean that, you know I don't," she sighed.

"I do know," Mellors responded. "But I have to leave thee. I had to bring these up to the house but I need to get back. There's been an accident in t' village. A young lad has got hisself caught in some machinery and he's done himself a damage. I'm bound to get down there and see if there's owt I can do."

"Oh, I'm sorry for that," Connie said. "Will he be alright?"

"He'll nay be alright for some things, I fear. He's been cut, like a gelding, I mean."

Why, what on earth do you mean?" Connie gasped. "Do you mean he's been castrated?"

"It happens to men of all classes, my lady."

Connie looked darkly at him. "That's a terrible thing to say. Didn't you say he was just a boy? What is his name, pray?"

117

"He's nobbut fifteen, my lady. Lad by t' name of Blackly."

"How did it happen, this terrible circumstance?"

"I'm not entirely sure, but I know he works in t' sawmill. I guess you can imagine what's took place."

She looked down as Mellors turned away and then she felt almost as saddened and gloomy about this brief encounter as for what had happened to the lad from the village. A violent emasculation and terrific loss, but she presumed he had never felt the ache of love at his tender age and therefore, she felt, what had happened did not necessarily outweigh her own privation. She walked ruminatively back into her private garden once more to attend to the odours of her flowers and to catch a last glimpse of the big purple heads of the upstanding celosia there.

THE TAILOR'S BOY

Listen carefully. It's not a long tale, but it's a tricky one. And I'll give it tongue presently. Ha! Give it tongue, that's a good one!

It starts, I suppose you'd consider, with me working at the tailor's down near Dartford. But it don't really start there, you see. It starts with a cobbler named Gaggs, a violent man I was prenticed to up in Bow three or four years earlier. He treated me like a animal, it has to be said. Made me eat my bread out in the yard at the back of his shop and never let me ask no questions or do nothing much to learn the cobbling trade that were his duty to have done so. I were raised a orphan, see, so I was shove out to work as soon as ever I could be shoved, and them as done the shoving didn't pay no heed to the direction of my propulsion, you might say. So I ended up with my master, Ezekiel Gaggs, a man who hated life in general and boys in particular, and both of 'em in about ekerval measure. And I ended up in a shop full of leather and awls and plenty enow hard surfaces to bump against when I were being bumped, or to lay my head on when I had a moment to lay it, which weren't that often, let me tell you.

But I exscaped. Now the manner of my exscape don't concern the present tale, but the reasons why I had to exscape do, so let me tell 'ee. As I say, I shan't be long about it. No, atcherly, I'll leave that for later. Anyway, I knowed I had to get away from London. I could have gone North, but that dint seem to make much sense, the folk up that way being a bit strange, to my sensing of things; or I could have gone West, but there's wild men in those parts, wilder than Gaggs even, mebbe. There ain't nothing much to the East of London, so it had to be downwards to the South. Accordingwise I made my way across to Greenwich and from there down the coast as far as Dartford, which I considered might have a bit of life to it, because of the sailors and that. It were a long old trudge but I made it in a single day and there I stopped for the night at a tavern called The Cock, thinking as I might try and get some employment in the town the next day. Just after midnight there was a bit of a rumpus though, involving one of the other guests and a young serving wench, so I used the occasion to slip away early in the morning, whiles everyone was still asleep, without having to pay for my lodging. I did have a few shillings that I had taken from old Gaggs by way of severance pay, as you might call it, but I knowed it weren't going to last forever. Dartford may have just a tad too much life about it, I were forced to concede, so I decided to move on.

And that's how I come to a little hamlet near Northfleet. It weren't more than two streets running parallel to their chuther; the one with a little row of shops – a tailor's, a corn chandler's, a baker's and so on – and the other one, which weren't no more than a track, running behind these establishments. There were an inn as well and a church further up the hill, St Botulph's I think it's called. It didn't look to be much of a place to make my fortun', but it were a long way from the Bow Street Runners and from Old Gaggs, so I thought to myself, 'This here will do for a lad who's footsore and ravenous.'

The first person I spoke to were an ostler. He was saying something to this rounded sort of a man who was wearing a fawn greatcoat, though it weren't all that cold. I waited for a while before interrupting, but this roundy sort just stood there as I was asking the stable lad where I might buy a morsel of bread or a pie to tide me through the day. The ostler jerked his thumb behind him at the inn, and then, when I looked a bit blank, pinted out the baker's, but Mr Trabb, as he later told me was his name, took me by the elbow and said if I'd come with him to his shop he could provide me with something in the way of wittles. And what was more, perhaps I'd care to do him the favour of having a brief conversation about something that might be of mutual benefit.

I didn't think it would harm to accompany him to the shop, which was only a short walk away, so that's what I did. As we walked he said, in a wheezy old voice like he he'd been pulling a cart up a great hill all his life, that he'd been in the tailoring trade for above twenty five years but

120

he was advancing into middle years now and might be thinking of getting some help in the shop. "I don't have a son to pass the business on to, you see," he said, "So I'm obliged to do all the fine work myself. I've no doubt that you, a young man of vigour, could be of use to me with some of the other duties in the shop, however."

I looked at him a bit suspicious, because of my recent dealings in the cobbling trade, but I spoke up. "Like what duties might you be thinking on?"

"Well, the cleaning and the tidying and the sorting. General work."

We stepped inside the shop and though it wasn't exactly bright in there it was neater and tidier than I were used to. Rows of teak shelves behind the counter, all stocked with rolls of twill and flannel and Egyptian cotton for shirtmaking. A plasterwork dummy and some rails with fine double breasted weskits hanging there. A bentwood chair for customers to take their ease during fittings. I have to admit I imagined myself having a good old sit down on that chair if things turned out the way things was looking to turn out. He saw me regarding the chair and he gave a sort of smile, then he looked serious again and he motioned me to foller him on through the shop into a parlour at the back, where he asked me to sit while he boiled a kettle and made us both a mug of tea. I sat down at a table where he did the sewing work, for these were the days before Mr Singer invented his automated sewing machine, and I took a good look around. He had a big old mantel clock made of what looked like gold but I guessed was brass, a stuffed parrot in a bamboo cage, and more rolls of cloth stacked against one wall. He caught me looking and smiled at me again.

"So what would the work consist of, exactly?" I said, trying to sound business-like.

"As I say, some cleaning and general work."

"So, it would be a matter of a broom ..."

"You would be furnished with a broom, of course."

"And would I be prenticed, or salaried, might I venture to ask?"

121

He looked down his nose at me, then removed his pince-nez coz they was in danger of falling off. "When I mentioned, as I did only a moment ago, I believe, that it was *general* work, I thought it would be understood that I do not intend to train a lad as a tailor. I require a boy to sweep and carry. Sweep and carry, my boy, that's the nature of the position. Now, do I want to work, and earn a day's honest living, or do I want to scavenge the countryside, *that* would be the right sort of question to be asking."

"I believe it is work that interests me, not starving," I said. "But might I be excused a certain boldness in my queries? I was rather badly treated by my last employer, you see, and I was just wishing to know where I stand, if I was to accept your kind offer of employment. Oh, and there would bed and board, I take it, in addition to a daily wage?"

"Why, you are a forrard sort of young un, aren't ee?" he said. "But as long as you hold your tongue in front of my customers, you will fare well enough, that's all I shall stipulate. As to board, you may take an evening meal with me here in my living quarters, though you'll have to fend for yourself as far as breakfast is concerned. You can buy yourself a loaf out of your wages, I daresay. And as for bed, there is a attic room yonder," he jerked his head up in the direction of the ceiling and this time his pince-nez, which he had returned to his nose for the sake of appearing professional and genteel, I suspect, fell completely off.

So, without much further ado, I accepted the job and set to sweeping and carrying, though in truth there weren't very much of the latter to be done, since cloth can only be moved about if there is any tailoring and cloth cutting getting done. And, times being what they were, there weren't much of anything associated with the bespoke tailoring business a-going on. That is, until we had a major order. And hereby hangs the tale, I might say.

A young man, no moren a couple of year older than I was, come in one day and it was this day's business that was the cause of all the harm that were to come about. I wasn't insolent or nothing; I just kind of hung around at the back of the shop as old Trabb fussed about the young man and measured him and dandled specimens in front of him and generally fawned all over the young toff. But when the gennelman, as I have to call him, on account of his pocketbook, I suppose, when the gennelman gave me a sideways look, Trabb cuffs me round the ear and says "Sweep, boy, sweep. You know what you get paid for."

So I swep. There weren't hardly no dust or cotton thread or nothing *to* sweep, but I made a darned good job of banging the brush around on the floor, I tell 'ee. I'm what you may call a digilent worker, you see. Trabb tutted and turned his attention back to the gennelman, who was looking at me with scorn in his narrow eyes. I noticed though he had a red apple blush about the cheeks, as if he'd just run half a mile. That made me smile, coz it showed he was new to the gentleman trade, and he seemed to know that I knew it were so too.

"Sweep all that outside," Trabb said to me. I had but a morsel of dust on the end of my brush, but I obeyed orders and I brushed my way past the customer and out into the street. Why should I mind? It weren't bad having a moment to sun myself out of doors, I thought. And that should have been an end to it. But it weren't.

It were some time after, and I'd pretty well forgotten about this jumped up young gent, this personage, when Trabb called me into his quarters as I was tidying up the shop at the end of the day. "So," he starts up, "You think you can ruin my trade, do you? Mmm? Speak up, boy!"

I didn't know what he were talking about. Then I see he had a letter in his right hand. He picked up his pince-nez and perched them on his flabby red nose. "This here is a letter, boy, in which you are mentioned by name."

Now I know the letter didn't mention *my* name, coz I never told anybody what my real name was. Not Trabb, not anybody. I said I was called Johnny when Trabb first asked me, coz I'd heard that was the name of a predecessor of mine at Gaggs' the cobbler's, but nobody else down here in Kent ever asked me my name, they just knew me as The Tailor's Boy. And that was fine and dandy where I was concerned.

"And you are mentioned in a light which I find most disagreeable,"

Trabb went on. "You have apparently been mocking your superiors and making light of the gentry. This is something what I should not tolerate in any boy, let alone a boy in the employ of yours truly. So, what do you have to say about it, eh?"

"I haven't got nothing to say, for I don't know what you are talking about, Mr Trabb, sir."

"Nothing to say, you profess? Well now, that's not what Mr Pip tells me in his correspondence."

"'Pon my soul, sir, I don't know a gentleman of that name," I cried. "Who is this Mr Pip who accuses me? And what, pray, do he accuse me of?"

"I will not stand for your insolence and impudence young man," Trabb burst out. "Here, put your hands on the back of this chair."

I didn't have a clue what he intended, but I put my hands on the chair as I was directed. It were like he was going to chastise me as the teachers do the pupils in schools, with his belt or a pandybat something. But I weren't afraid or nothing. I guess I was about the same stature, or height any road, as Trabb himself at this time, not some whimpering, simpering chitling. I was still cogitating the likely outcome of events when the old man whipped a piece of cloth round my wrists and, quick as a sailor, fashioned a knot that any tar would have been proud of as he tied me to the chair.

"We have ways to stop young whippersnappers from abusing their betters, and *my customers*," he roared. I didn't see what he did next, for he turned his back to me for a moment. Then his face was in mine, just an inch or two away, and I suddenly felt a searing pain bolt through my lower lip. I tried remonstrating, but he had caught my nose in a pinching, twisting motion and all that came out was a gargled groaning, like what an animal might utter when he's caught in a trap. Then a second pain, as sharp as anything I've ever felt, as he stabbed through my tongue with a four inch darning needle. He pushed the needle right up through and above my upper lip, where I had hoped to grow a moustache as soon as ever I might be able. Then it finally dawned on me what was happening

124

to me. I had scarcely struggled at first, so deft had Trabb been with his instant stitching, though now I kicked out in rage and pain but all I achieved was to send myself and the chair I was bound to crashing to the floor.

"You see, I've had to sew your lip, young man. Now let that be a lesson." Trabb looked a little bit astonished himself at what he had perpetrated. There must have been a fair amount of blood. I don't know, I passed out, and Trabb had to do some floor cleaning for himself for once.

The yarn was gone when I come to, though my lips and tongue were stinging like a thousand bees had had an almighty row in my mouth. When I looked in a glass it didn't look all that serious either. There was a prick hole just below my lower lip and just above my upper lip, but my tongue just looked a bit redder than usual. Of course it was swoll up something horrendous. But that was just that night.

Trabb didn't say nothing further. At some point he put a bowl of meat and cabbage down in front of me and I managed to eat a bit of it, albeit with considerable caution and not a little pain. But trying to slip the wittles past that thick lump of tongue I could feel filling my mouth was too hard to continue with, however hungry I might have been. Atcherly, I don't recall being that ravenous, to tell the truth, I was just completely exhausted and I was glad enough to make my way to my attic room as soon as ever I could.

The next day Trabb had to get the doctor in. My face had blown up puffier than a marsh toad and my tongue had turned a colour you aren't supposed to see in a man's face, lest it be the eyes of course, for it were a dark green hue. I couldn't really see this, it just looked dark to me, but I had to use the back of a spoon I had in my room to undertake my oral investigations, there being no glass for me to use. "You 'd only preen and prevaricate in front of one, if I furnished you with a glass," Trabb said to me once.

The doctor tried not to hurt me, but he failed in that. He did give me a potion howsomever, which I noticed Trabb paid for without a murmur, and that subdued the worst of the fearsome ache in my mouth.

And he came back to see me a further twice, or thrice, it may have been. "The swelling has abated somewhat," I hear him telling old Trabb, "But I fear the tongue is out of joint, as it were."

Trabb said something I couldn't catch, then the doctor turned to me. "Now listen, young man," he said. "You are not going to die, and you will be up and about and tending to your business in a very short time." He looked at Trabb and so did I at that point. We both must have been thinking, tend to Trabb's business, more like. "But you may experience some difficulty in using your vocal apparatus for the foreseeable future. That is to say, you may not be able to make yourself understood perfectly clearly. Nod if you understand what I am saying to you, would you, young sir?"

I nodded, but it hurt to do so. Trabb nodded furiously, as if on my behalf.

"That's good then," the doctor said. "Now, let's not be having any more silly sewing accidents, eh?"

I saw that Trabb had been economical with the truth of my 'accident'. Even if I could have argued the case, however, I knew there would be little point. The doctor had received his moneys and he was in no hurry to stay in my cramped room for a moment longer than was absolutely necessary.

It was several days before I felt well enough to return to work, and even then old Trabb did not demand much of me. He went about his business in a far less bumptious way than of yore, and seemed reluctant to look my way most of the time, perhaps for fear of the remonstrances I might have offered him, if I could have talked properly. As to that, I could only summon up a sort of gruff barking noise by way of communication, for my tongue had grown misshapen and would not do my bidding when I tried to speak. For my part, I glowered at him, but mainly at his back, and contented myself with my lighter workload.

For the first few days Trabb gave me gruel for my evening meal, recognising that I would have difficulty chewing meat, but on the fourth day of this unsatisfying regime I grunted and barked that I needed something more wholesome. He came to understand by my gestures towards his plate of chops that I was at least recovered enough to be fed like a young man, for that was what I now termed myself, and not like a cur, and, though he said nothing, he allowed me a proper share of the next day's liver and onion casserole that he had brought in from The Blue Boar.

The months went by and Trabb seemed to decline into a lethargy and a carelessness about his whole existence, let alone his tailoring business. During this time, though no words of tuition or encouragement passed between us, I began to learn some of the finer points about the cutting of cloth and the sewing of seams. My dexterity with the needle brought me increasing satisfaction, though I doubt it consoled old Trabb too much, despite the fact that it saved him some work. Little did he know that I had been treated much worse by my former master Ezekiel Gaggs.

And, though it pains me to have to tell this part of my tale, for there is no way I can express what happened with any sort of delicacy, it is at this point that I feel I have to confess what happened in London. Gaggs was a Jew, but he must have had a bit of the Greek in him, for he was, how shall I say it, no lover of women. I believe I was always a vivacious and sprightly sort of boy, and mayhap lissom in form, though I prefer to think of myself as wiry. I know I have, or any road had, a catching sort of smile and what might be called a twinkle in my eye. You must know what I am trying to say. But I am not a eunuch or a catamite; I hoped to grow into a full, virile chap what the ladies would find appealing. Gaggs had no interest in me becoming anything of the sort, however. He sought to possess me like a gennelman does a serving wench, by which I meantersay he bought me little treats and paid me blandishments, all the time plotting the dastardly acts he were going to perpetrate on me. I thought these kindly words were intended to encourage me in my cobbling skills, but it turned out he had a different motive. He came to the cot in the back of the shop after dark one night and threw himself upon me. There, I've admitted it. I was too little and too weak to resist his loathsome advances and, though I sobbed with indignation and with actual physical pain, he made me his thing, his creature, for the whole of

127

the night. I wanted to take up a bludgeon and kill him, but I knew he were too strong and too wily for me, so I planned a different course of action. I said nothing during the course of the whole next day, but I'd worked out a design to get my revenge. I waited till Gaggs took his regular midday nap and I stacked up a pile of straw from the outhouse outside his bedroom door. I already had a flint and steel which I'd palmed from the mantel where the old man kept them and, almost to my own surprise, I was able to set a healthy fire within a few seconds. I stood on the landing and watched in a mixture of glee and awe as the flames licked at his door but I still half thought the old man would come tumbling out of the room, awoked by the fumes, at any moment. But he still lay fast asleep, exhausted, no doubt, by the previous night's exertions. I could hear his heavy slumberous breathing through a crack in the door. When I was certain that he was not about to emerge, I ran down the stairs, each one of them groaning that there were a boy excsaping from some terrible crime, and pausing only to help myself to some wages in lieu, I bolted out of the front door of the shop into the street. And that's how I come to leave the cobbling trade.

Now, with Trabb apparently discomfited and scarcely interested in his own trade, I felt that I had some measure of power in the shop, and I took to tailoring with a will, as you might say. When folk came in to order a weskit or pair of trews it was me what made 'em, though of course it was up to Mr Trabb to do the talking with the customer, me being still pretty mutified by what my guvnor had done to me.

Time passed as it do pass, then one day I saw my nemesis, the so-called gennelman Mr Pip, once more. He were wearing London clothes of course, so he had no business at my shop, but I thought he looked a little distressed, despite his fine apparel.

"Is your master about?" he said, his voice lowered as if he might be afeared he might be overheard, though there weren't nobody in the shop but me.

"He's taking a nap, sir," I rejoined, though I have to say the 'sir' came out of me surly enough, if I'm permitted a pun. By this time I could talk again, but in a thick sort of way as if my words were coming through a hedge.

"It's Trabb's boy, ain't it?" he added.

"What do have a name," I said, but he weren't paying much attention, fumbling for something in his jacket pockets as he was.

"I need to get out to the lime kiln this evening and I've neglected to bring a greatcoat," he said, almost as if he were talking to himself. "I was wondering if I could borrow something sturdier to wear, for it looks to be a dank enough night,"

"You can take my coat," I said, surprising myself with the offer. "It's a-hanging up there on the hook over your head. But you'll not do your 'ealth any good wandering across the meshes in this weather."

He looked without looking, if you know what I mean, and mumbled something else which I couldn't catch, and then he just turned on his heels and walked out of the shop. Now you may be a-wondering why I was so ready to help the gennelman. I sometimes wonder myself, but I suppose it's because I somehow recognised that we weren't so very different really, despite him having come into money. We both come from poor backgrounds and we both just done what we could with what we had, or dint have, when it's all said and done. I don't know, I just thought it would be the right thing to do, to put a piece of cloth on a person's back when they might get cold. Taint so very much to do, in the big scheme of things.

I saw him again an hour or two later, after I had shut up the shop and was thinking of taking myself to the inn for a dash of something a little vivifying. He was bustling out of the Blue Boar, still without a coat, I noticed. He set off down the High Street but not in the direction of the forge, which I know were where he was brought up. Doubtless he intended to get to the kiln a quicker way.

He were not long gone when two of his gennelmen friends showed up in the Blue Boar, one of them brandishing a letter. I heard them asking the potboy if he'd seen a London gentleman that evening but the lad shrugged, so I thought I'd help out, though there weren't no benefit for me in it.

"He went that way," I said, pointing, "He's headed for the lime kiln."

The two gentlemen looked blank.

"Come on then," I said, "I'll have to show ye."

We set out toward old Gargery's forge and then stumbled across the meshes as rapid as we could, all of us perhaps sensing some sort of new urgency, though no one said nothing, till we saw a light in the abandoned sluice house up ahead. Then suddenly a fearful shouting came from inside and two silhouettes could be seen through the grimy winderpane. I heaved against the stiff, rotting door and there were Mr Pip, cowering against a stove and Orlick, the former gatekeeper at Satis House, standing over him with a stonecutter's hammer clenched in his big paw. One of the gennelmen (name of Pocket, I heard later) threw hisself at Orlick and wrested the hammer off of him. The other young man was beating with both hands on Orlick's back and trying to get him to the ground, but rather more in the manner of a wench in a cat fight than a proper manly attack. I stepped up and swung a mighty blow at his head, which caught him full on the side of the jaw, and Orlick collapsed in a heap of young men. It hurt my knuckles a tad, but it were satisfying I have to say, though I didn't bear no particular grudge agin the man. He wasn't the most sociable of types but he never done me no harm.

The two young men were bent down over Orlick's intended wictim, for he had swooned or something, saying "Pip, Pip," as if he were like to die or something. I thought he looked rather pale, and I said as much, though I can't say my 's's no more and it come out as 'lookth' as if I were a lisping eight year old.

And that were about the end of it, as far as the drama goes. I never saw Mr Pip again arter that night, though I believe his story were told to a writer, who put it all down in big fancy words in a book some time later. No one ever really found out what was irking Old Orlick so much that he wanted to take the gennelman's life like that. He were most probably envious that Mr Pip come to be so wealthy, as he done, fortuitous like. I do believe he never got to enjoy his riches though, the government taking it all off of him apparently, for some reason.

But my story's more normal. I took over the shop after Trabb died, which weren't long after the events I just told you about. And I done alright. I can cut up pieces of cloth, and I can sew a fine garment, but I haven't got the gift of cutting up bits of story and sewing them into a right pleasing shape, I suppose. You've got to have a pattern, see? And my life just doesn't seem to have such a thing. What happened to me perchance happens to more young folk than you'd care to imagine, but there's a difference between a needle and a pen, and I can't sew round the holes in my story like it were a buttonhole. I suppose I could say that I did find a bit of my voice after all, despite Trabb's efforts at silencing me, but no one's going to read these pages, are they? Or at least not till years and years after I've gone before.

NO NEED TO TALK

It's all senses when you're this age. The warm smells, the soft tastes, the firm yet gentle touch. Nothing much to see yet, and no great refinement that allows distinction of the various sounds that fill the cloying air. I try to speak, to utter what I do not know but yet I feel, but consonants and vowels blur; my tensile tongue cannot flick back and forth as others' seem to do. I lie and stare at shapes and shapeless forms. The days rock by like clouds. The one who tends coos at my oval face and moves around and out of sight. And so it goes.

I like my body. I like its plenitude, its smooth uncomplicatedness. I know it all, despite the clothes, the vests, the blankets, all the layers of care they foist upon me. My legs are pliant jelly sausages, my arms the same. It's almost as if I have no bones. I test a digit – smooth and tasteless – but strangely satisfying. I flex a hand, my fingers frond and splay. I could do this all summer's day, but something grips my gut and I surprise myself with the sudden sound that bursts from me. A one comes running, swoops her bony arms and grabs me up. I fly through the thick, unseemly air to land upon her where the smell is strongest. There I stare at her and watch her flying tongue, attend to the big lips and strange unwieldy teeth. She makes a sound that means nothing yet to me. It sounds like leaves or the shushing of the rain.

At other times there is a larger one. The smell is different and the grip and grasp a tighter one. This other stares at me and does not seem to recognise whatever it is he sees. I writhe or slump or stretch, according to mood. He does not hold me long. There are others too; shadowy forms that move around like birds, inspecting this, discarding that, cawing their disagreement, their dissatisfaction, then flying away to land on something else. Their needs are different, I sense, and I wonder how I'll come to this. At present all I think is here I am, whatever I am, and here will do. No, more than that, I like this thisness – haecceitas is all. I sense they do not understand, despite their protestations about knowing everything and feeling more.

The warm sun filters through the leaves of the two oak trees in the front yard and I smell jasmine and mimosa as a slight gust of wind rattles the shutters. But the scent is soon overwhelmed by a syrupy aroma that wafts into this room where I spend my daylight hours. It comes from a room somewhere at the back of the house. I have never seen this room, but it is from there that most of the sounds and smells of the house emanate. I have learned already to distinguish between certain sensations. Just a short while ago I could be alarmed by a yelp or cry from a child running past the porch or soothed by the pip-pip-pip of a motor out on the street. Now I know that these sounds are not part of my immediate world. Other noises – the creak of a step, the wheeze of a drawer, a cupboard door closing with a click or an upstairs door being banged shut – belong to me. At this moment I can hear the sounds familiar to this part of the day when I am newly awake. A metal sound. A sound of china. The scrape of wood on a stone floor. A high shrill screech that subsides to a whistling sigh. It reminds me of the birds I hear at times, but this is no bird, for the sound is too sad.

And it is the same with the sensations that assail my nostrils. There are the inside smells and the different, more pungent aromas I detect when I am lying in my carriage on the front porch and someone passes by. Sometimes the scent is rich and flowery, but not the scent of an actual flower, more the essence of a whole bouquet of lilac or lavender. Other times it is acrid like burning leaves, or dense and thick like molasses, with a yeasty fragrance. I smell that human waft of heat and fatigue too. I am propped up on a lacy pillow but I cannot see the forms that pass, though I sense that they hurry by the house and show no acknowledgement of the shadowy shapes of the ones inside.

I drift in and out of sleep, content enough for the most part, though occasionally I am gripped by a pain in my lower parts. When this happens I surprise myself with the force of my cries and the strength of my small body as I arch my back and flail at the unfair world. Not even the large black hands of the one who lifts me out of my bed can hold me still until I find myself thrown over a shoulder and my pain subsides. I nestle into the rough calico of this shoulder and allow a huge flat palm to tap and rub at my back. This one is different from the other ones. She sings softly to me in a mellow contralto, continuing to pat me long after the ache in my stomach has gone. The song is of the big wide river. Then she lays me on a cool surface somewhere and I feel the coolness of the air in a darkened room as it brushes my thighs and loins. She lets me wave my fat legs around and kick at the heavy air for a while before wrapping me up again, a clean gift to the other ones.

One day these things will change. The black one will disappear and tend to other cries in another house. I will see and recognise the forms that move around the house and know the voices of Nathan and my parents. I will respond to the name they have given me, though I will know too that I am called by a different name by the children who hurry past the house. I will try to speak their language, that lilt of sounds that alternately seems to drawl and then slip and slide over consonants like oil over metal. Somehow I know that it should be my language too, but I also feel that I will spurn it and communicate by gesture and action alone. The man who is in charge of my destiny, he of the too tight grip and the musty smell, will intone from a big black book and I will not respond to the words. He will punish me and say that he is protecting me. The woman will not deter him. Neither will my brother. They have certainties and will not accept that things could be any different. They do not sense the world in the perfumy, tactile way that I do.

I will play like the other children of course, at least in those short periods of time when I am freed into a nearby schoolyard, but I will merely whoop and hail as I chase, or breathe in a hoarse fear, but as silently as I can, when I hide. When I am back in the house such frivolities as running or climbing or bowling a hoop will be strictly forbidden and I will be left alone for long stretches to colour or cut out paper shapes. Then meals will be eaten in silence after the tedious thanking of a deity whose presence darkens the home like a shroud. As night descends mother will embroider and father will read the newspaper or more often murmur long passages from the black book. Nathan is a lot older than me. He is waiting to become my father.

I will lurch into adolescence like a car running off the road into a ditch and I will flounder there in that dirty water for years, but I will not call for help. By the time anyone attends to my flailing limbs I will already be regarded as beyond help. But I will be saved by my family. And my saving will be my punishment. The aromas from the porch and the pavement outside will be blocked off by the flaking shutters on the windows. The sounds of life from the neighbouring houses and the thrum of gossip and news from the street corner and the step outside the post office will be muted and as distant as the days when I aired my tiny limbs in the sun. I will spend my days chopping up words from father's discarded papers, trying out new languages. The scissors will be my stick and hoop.

And the years will pass. It took five long summers and five long winters for the old century to grind into the new one. Now three decades and more have passed like engines racing to a fire. But now once again I can hear and smell what it is like to be alive, or at least what it is like for the others to be so.

I am thirty seven years old and I am no longer allowed the scissors. It is summer and the children from the house nearby do not pass by the porch on their way to school. They do sometimes tarry by the lamppost, but they seem to smell the decay and melancholy of our lives inside and they speak in low voices and only look furtively up at our windows. I see this as I peep past the edge of a curtain in my room. Then today, something new. They are planning something daring. The small boy is shaking his head and the girl is remonstrating with the one who is, I consider, her brother. I wait breathless and expectant but it still takes me by surprise when the leader of the little gang suddenly darts forward and bursts through the picket gate and dives up the dusty front path. He places a grubby hand on the wall and turns back, all in one swooping movement, and hurtles back to the safety of the sidewalk. He has not really tommy-knocked; he has scarcely made a sound, but he is smiling now, triumphant at his daring act, and the small one and the girl are thrilled and impressed, I can tell. I move quickly away from my window as they look up. This is the first time I can recall a child entering our garden. Dr Reynolds is the only person who ever comes to the house and even the mailman takes as little time as possible sliding a letter into our box by the front gate, the few times he needs to. But I can say to myself now that I have had a visitor. I shall pay the boy the due courtesy and acknowledge his kindness.

***

Last night I crept out when Father and mother were asleep. I only had some chewing gum that I was saving. Two sticks. I wished I'd kept a whole package but I wanted to respond to the visit and give the children something. I placed the slim pieces in a knot hole in one of the oak trees, taking care to leave an edge of the silver foil showing. A grownup would not notice it; their eyes operate at a different level, but a child, alert to its environment like a cat or a dog, might spot it the first time it passed by the tree trunk. And so it transpired. It was the girl. She reached up and examined what she'd found, glancing round nervously in case she'd been seen. She hesitated, but then stuffed her treasure into the pocket of her dungarees. I hope she is allowed gum.

Now I have something to look forward to the time drags more slowly than ever. Before the children paid me their courtesy, days melted into weeks like raindrops sliding into rivulets on my window. Since the boy, who is called Gem because he is so sharp and clear and beautiful, like a diamond, since the boy came to me, the hours are like stones I am trying to roll up a steep street. I while the time away listening to the birds and to the birdlike women gossiping on the street. I do not attend to their talk, for it is as meaningless to me as the chirrup of the mockingbirds, but I know what they are talking about from the expression on their faces as a negro walks by on the other side of the street. They cast their eyes down, then heavenward, and they tug at their shawl or scrape a talon through their slick grey hair. They fall quiet for the time it takes for the negro to pass out of earshot, then they take up their clacking and chirruping once again. I do not know why they feel this way towards the black man, with his bowed head and slouching gait.

And now it is summer again. The pecans are blossoming in the back yard, though we do not eat of the tree. Perhaps Gem and the girl will pause by the lamppost and play their games of conspiracy and acting. Their friend who comes in the summer, like a visiting purple martin or barn swallow, might come back one of these days too. He is a small bright child who has two names, the one the boy and girl use and the one the adults use. I prefer his child name because it reminds me of the aroma of herbs. When we had a cook I would frequently smell oregano and chicory and dill and rosemary, but since Father has been ill and we no longer have servants Mother only prepares plain food. She says the lord provides, but in truth he seems to provide only the barest of essentials. Father has taken to eating his meals in his bedroom, so Mother, Nathan and I eat supper in grave silence in the kitchen. I cannot wait to get it over with so I can go back upstairs and watch from my window.

And tonight they are back, the children. They are arguing by the lamp post, Gem fidgeting and moving from foot to foot, the girl leaning on a sort of broom or besom she has fashioned from a branch and some twigs. I do not attend to the snatches of talk but watch their gestures instead, like I am a meerkat or some such creature. I want to offer them a gift again, to show them that I understand what it is like to be remote from the adult world and to live a life of dreams and play.

I know it is wrong to have graven images but I have two Indian pennies that I keep in my box of treasures. On one side is a fine noble Indian in full head dress with the word 'Liberty' printed on it. The other side tells you how much the coin is worth and there is a sort of wreath made of oak leaves and strips of olive tree around the words. The coins are not heavy but I like the feel of them and the coppery colour of them too. I tried cleaning them in water at first but they are old, one of them over thirty years old, and they would not recover their gloss and glow. Then, after I had seen Mother wiping a copper kettle with a rag soaked in vinegar, I tried soaking the coins in a dish with some vinegar I had purloined from the kitchen. The dirt and age faded away like a winter morning mist and I watched in awe as they were restored to the freshness and brightness of their earliest days. But then I had to quickly take them out because I was afraid the pennies would melt completely.

I have decided to offer my treasure to the children. It is a shame that I don't have a third coin, for the boy Dill, but he has not migrated North to our lands yet and he is just a visitor after all, I reason. I place the shining one cent pieces in a ring box of rose taffeta that I have taken from Mother's dressing table drawer and I wrap the box in tinfoil. When it is dark and the street is completely still and quiet I slip out of the front door and put the gift in the oak tree knot hole. I will watch from behind the shutter and see their delight tomorrow or the next day or whenever it is they see that their friend has remembered them.

They found the box. They were nervous and excited and argued, I think over who should accept the present, but I mean that they should have one coin each, the older for Gem, because he is older himself, and the shinier one for the girl, because she is bright like the morning sun. And it is good that they made their discovery just in time, before their friend arrived, for he is back now and might have been jealous.

It is Tuesday, I think, and the sun is high, though I have only been at my post watching for signs of life for a couple of hours. The children, an unruly triumvirate again, are arguing about what happened yesterday, when the girl was being pushed along the sidewalk inside a tyre and she came crashing into our front yard. She fell out of the great tube and staggered back out onto the street looking abashed and dirty, and even more confused when Gem started shouting at her. I could guess his meaning when he shrugged in exasperation and rushed in to drag the tyre back out onto the sidewalk. I think they know that what might offend Mother and father is the noise, the life, the hectic motion. Nobody moves quickly in my house and only Father's coughing disturbs the somnolence. We are mute, dead servants of the lord.

It is another day; it doesn't matter which day of the week, but it is not Sunday. That day of rest is a day of torment for me, for Nathan stays at home now Father is too unwell to go to church. He reads from the testaments in his deep ponderous voice and rebukes me when it is plain I am not listening. Today the children were told off by the lawyer man, the father, but it was a different type of rebuke from Nathan's remonstrations. They speak back. They had been squatting on the sidewalk clipping stories from newspapers, I guess to provide material for their little plays that they like to act for me. They complained that they were doing no harm and I couldn't see how they could have been, but they were made to go back indoors anyway.

But they are back. The boy Gem is trying to give me a note. They can't see me behind the shutters and I am afraid to move in case they scare and run away. I hold my breath till I'm fit to bursting as I watch the fluttering sheet of paper that they've stabbed through and is now on the end of a long bamboo stick. The pole is too flexible though and it's just waving about out of reach of the side window shutter that Gem is trying to post it through. The little girl is excited, barely able to control herself as she tries to encourage her brother and spur him on. Dill is looking more nervous, darting his head back and forth up and down the street. And then I see why. He has a dinner bell like the one on the great sideboard that we never use, and he is ringing it furiously. He is still shaking it when their father appears, slowly taking off his spectacles and wiping them on a handkerchief he has pulled from his pocket. He says something to Dill and the boy drops his hand and lowers his head. Gem has given up in his attempt to post me his note and he looks like he's trying to think of a story to tell that would explain why he is fishing where there is no water. The girl doesn't look afraid, however. She is staring straight up into the old man's face and saying something. I think there is even a wry sort of smile on his face as he listens, but he holds his hand up to stop her and then he takes the pole off them and shepherds them back up the street. I wonder what was in the note. I wonder if they realise I wouldn't hardly know what to make of their words.

***

The seasons aren't the same as they used to be. I used to scarcely be aware of days and weeks passing and leaves and berries forming on the skeletons of trees; summer seemed to last forever, the heat of the days stretching into late evening; autumn never arrived with any drama of wind or rainfall, though after a while I'd be aware that it had been lurking for some time in the shadows of the pecan trees. It's different now; it's

139

early September, but today is one of those days when everything is paused because tonight or tomorrow Autumn will boldly shove Summer aside. The children seem to be aware of it too, though in a way I never was when I was their age. I think they're upset somehow. I guess they know about change the way animals know it. Birds get together to fly off and they can just sense when it's time to quit. Which reminds me that Dill will be going home any day now, I guess. Perhaps that's what's making them feel so wound up tight.

From my vantage point by the window at the top of the stairs I see them in the school grounds where they back on to our vegetable garden. I rarely see them here; it's as if they are glad to be away from school when they can be. They are mooching about wordlessly, though Gem pauses by the wire fence that separates the schoolyard from our overgrown collard patch. There's no way I can tell what's in his mind though.

And today I know what he must have been thinking, after the momentous events of last night. I don't think Nathan meant to harm the children though. Nevertheless, they must have been terrified. I wish I'd seen them creeping up to the back porch, an Indian file of naughtiness, but I was looking out of my window at the front of the house when I heard the shotgun go off. I hurried down the corridor to the rear window and was in time to see Dill and the little girl rolling their little bodies under the wire fence. At first, I couldn't see Gem and I was shocked at the idea that he wasn't there; this looked like a major piece of daring, creeping into our backyard. Then I saw him struggling at the base of the fence. As I was staring, amazed at what I was witnessing, I heard the cocking of the second barrel of the shotgun and it was then that I saw the tall shadow of my brother spreading out from the porch in the pale moonlight. He wasn't aiming the gun though, he was cradling it in his arms like a puppy. Nathan never said nothing; he just stood there looking out toward the rows of cabbages that we don't tend any more. Not since Mother got ill. Gem must have heard the clicking of the gun too because he frantically pulled off his britches and hurtled off into the darkness. He'd got himself caught in the wire, I now realised, and it was tearing his pants. I watched for another twenty minutes or more, but there was nothing else to see. Nathan went back indoors and the children just slipped into the dark world beyond our lot.

I don't need sleep if I decide I don't want it. Or rather, I don't have to go to bed at a set time because I can catch naps any time of the day. Clearly, I wasn't set on going to bed now, so I waited, as I say, for about twenty minutes. Then I went back to my bedroom to look out and see if anyone had been roused by the noise of the shotgun. They certainly had. There was a whole bunch of people standing on the sidewalk, but they were starting to drift away by this time. I wished I'd had the sense to hurry to the front window sooner, to catch everyone around congregating just outside our house like this, but I was there in time to see Gem and the girl being questioned by the lawyer man, their father. Dill was saying something too and the grownups seemed satisfied with whatever he had said to explain their presence, and the fact that Gem was only wearing shorts. It was at this point I decided on my plan.

I waited another hour or so then I crept downstairs, avoiding the third step from the bottom. Slowly and carefully I raised the back door latch and peered out into the night. I knew the door might swing shut in the cool breeze that was up now, so I rolled up my handkerchief into a tight wad and put it on the jamb. That way there wouldn't be no tell-tale banging. Then I went and fetched the denim trousers that were snagged on the fence and took them back to my room. There was more furtive creeping to do because I had to get some yarn and a needle from Mother's sewing box in the rear sitting room, but the house was silent and heedless of my movements. My heart was still beating in my chest like a marching band though. I'd never sewed anything before so it took a while to mend the tear in Gem's pants, but I managed it somehow, and I must say I did a pretty fine job of it too. I knew it wasn't invisible mending, like I saw in an advert in a magazine once, but it would be appreciated, I felt. Accordingly, I felt pretty proud as I replaced the pants, neatly folded now, on the top wire of the fence. I didn't know when he'd come, but I was certain Gem would reclaim them soon enough. And so he did, creeping up to where they were with all the stealth of a fox. He paused, more like a deer now, sniffing the air, then all of a sudden he ran off with his prize like a gundog with a rabbit.

I didn't want the children to think that Mother had done the mending, or worse that Nathan had regretted firing into the air and scaring them like he'd done and was making up for it by sewing up Gem's pants. But I didn't think they'd see that it had to be my doing. Not until I came up with the idea of telling them, that is. And how could I tell them? Obvious, put the ball of twine I'd used for the fixing in the hole in the tree outside. They were the only souls who ever noticed the things I left there. So I pushed the ball of grey thread into that hole and went to bed contented. Mother would never notice it was gone; she was always in her bedroom these days.

There was something else that I took from Mother's box of things too. It was a cake of soap. At first, I didn't know why, it was just the lilac smell that made me want it, I think. Then when I took the soap out of its crinkly paper wrapping, I had an idea. Immediately I went back and took the other bar. These soaps were too good for washing, that's maybe why Mother had never used them. But they were beautiful to touch, soft and smooth like new skin. I took the pair of scissors that I still kept under my bed and began shaving at the first bar of soap. The flakes came off in curls, like wood shavings, and it was easy work to fashion a miniature figure, though fine details were obviously harder to sculpt. It took me over a week, but I managed to carve and press the cakes into two recognisable human shapes, one of Gem and one of his sister. It felt like I'd made a golem, two golems, and they'd burst into life. I was as happy as I've ever been.

They must have taken them, but I missed seeing it happen, which was a shame. I would have liked to see the expressions on their faces when they recognised themselves. If they did, that is. The soap bars were too small for fine detail, but I tried to suggest that one figure was a girl by giving it a skirt, though of course I've only ever seen Miss Finch wearing dungarees. I also gave her short hair with bangs, whilst the boy golem had a lick of hair coming down over his forehead, like Gem's does. It's hard to get across character though. If they'd been really true to life they would have been running or jumping figures, but I would have needed a lot more soap for that.

I also gave away my medal. It was nothing. Just a piece of metal. I don't care for words anymore, so the idea of having a sign that you were once good at them, or spelling them at least, struck me as just foolish. I thought Gem might think it was a medal that a soldier might have won in a war or something, except it never had a ribbon. That was the only piece of treasure I had left, but it would have been better if I could have presented it, like an honour at some ceremonious occasion. I wanted them to both have it though, and I'm not the type of person who could award medals anyway, so naturally all I could do was sneak out in the dead of the night and place it in the treasure hole. Once again, I didn't see them taking it out, sadly. I started to get afraid that I wouldn't see the children again, because the nights were drawing in and all. They rarely come down the street or hang around outside the house, now that winter is beginning to grip the town.

I grew desperate trying to think of just one last gift, one that might let them know it was me that was their unknown friend all this time, but there was nothing I could do. Until I went into Nathan's room yesterday, that is. Nathan is a very fastidious man and he keeps his room immaculately clean and tidy, so I thought it was pretty unlikely I'd find something there that he wouldn't miss. But, as I say, I was desperate. There were some brushes on the dressing table and some collars and studs in the drawer beneath, but no sign of a book or a magazine, or anything that might appeal to Gem or his sister. The only thing that I did find was an old watch and chain in a drawer of the nightstand. It was grandfather's watch and it didn't work, even though I tried winding it up. I nearly put it back, but there was a tiny knife attached to the chain, the kind you might use to do something intricate, like unscrewing the back plate, I guess. Boys like knives, they're dangerous. A girl like Miss Finch might like one too, I considered, she being such a tomboy. I slipped the watch into the pocket of my dressing gown and went back to my room. It took me all day to pluck up enough courage to decide that I would offer it as my final gift, however. If Nathan discovered that I had been tiptoeing round the house stealing the family's treasures, just to give them away to strangers, he'd go mad. But I had to do something.

I saw Gem taking my gift from the tree today. A wave of relief went through me, but also a wave of fear, because he looked up at my window as he was running the chain through his fingers. I knew he couldn't see me, but it was strange thinking that he perhaps knew finally where the gifts were coming from. People write cards when they give presents for birthdays or at Christmas; they want you to know the present's from them. I think for them it's about getting the satisfaction that people know what trouble you've gone to. And I suppose that's true of me too, except I only want to see the expression on their faces. I wouldn't want a speech, or even a thank you letter.

***

Father is dying. No one has said anything to me about it, but I overheard Nathan and Dr Reynolds talking in low, serious voices and I saw the doctor shaking his head as he went out of the house today. Mother may not know she's about to be widowed, because she doesn't come out of her bedroom any more, or it may be that she is past caring. She should be able to smell it though. I don't mean smell death itself, that hasn't got a particular aroma. I mean the camphor, or whatever medication Dr Reynolds has prescribed. The house smells different, I'm trying to say. I don't particularly feel anything about Father dying either, I have to confess. Nathan has become my father anyway. He cemented up the hole in the tree last week. I saw him mixing up some stuff as I was looking out of the rear window, but I didn't see what it was and I didn't know what he was planning. Something about the grim look on his face as he went round the side of the house made me go back to my bedroom window though. And then I instantly realised what he was doing. I was a little sad, but I don't have anything else to give, like I said, so it doesn't matter so much.

I said I had nothing to give, but tonight I was able to do something. And it was better than offering an old penny or a stick of chewing gum. It was wrapping a blanket round Miss Finch's shoulders to stop her shivering in the night air. She was out on the sidewalk, like the whole town, because there was a commotion down the street, with fire trucks and everyone rushing back and forth with buckets of water. All because there was a fire in one of the houses. I would have liked to watch the fire

144

because there's something grand about flames licking at wood and soaring through open windows, but at first I was too afraid to leave the house. I assumed Nathan was out there on the sidewalk too, so at first I just looked out of my window. Then I thought he might be too busy to notice me, so I crept out of the house. I even went through the front door. There was no sign of my brother anywhere, but I saw Miss Finch just outside our gate, trembling with cold because she had nothing on but a flimsy piece of cotton. I walked back in the house, bold as a fox, and got down a blanket from the box in the upstairs hallway. Then I went and put it round the poor little girl's shoulders. The fire was dying out by now and people were starting to turn back to their own business, so I had to slip away again. I doubt she even noticed me by her side.

And that all happened last year. Father duly died, and Mother followed in the Spring. Buds were forming on the pecan trees and the days were mellower. Light began to shimmer, as it does in the new season. The children were older now and it seemed that our brief affair was over. I stayed in my room a good deal, like I was turning into Mother.

Now it's a year since I did that thing with the blanket. Nothing much has happened in our inconsequential little town. The lawyer man shot a mad dog. A truck full of farmers carrying shotguns and such drove up the street, the men calling out and making a roistering din. They drove back quietly a short time after, so nothing could have gone off that meant anything. But tonight something did happen.

I killed a man.

It's as plain as that, in one way. A drunken man in frayed denims and a dirty red plaid shirt attacked a neighbour of mine, a young boy, and I grabbed him, knocked the knife he was brandishing out of his hand, and stabbed him through the heart. I had my own knife, a long blade I'd taken from the kitchen drawer. If I'd had to go to court about it there wouldn't have been much else I could have said, I don't suppose. I could have added that I'd seen the man following the children and knew that they were in danger, but most likely I wouldn't have been believed. But they didn't take me to court. Instead the lawyer man called at our house,

145

spoke to Nathan, and then led me over to the Finch house. I was taken into a room where Gem was lying in bed with his arm strapped up. They talked about the dead man and about what must have happened, but I wasn't listening. I stayed in the corner of the room, leaning against a wall in the shadows, too intent on being in the children's own house to think about anything. No one seemed to pay me much heed until little Jean Louise, as she's called, said howdy to me and called me by the name I used to have at school. Her father told her to use my real name and she did, but it sounded strange on her lips. Then I was led out onto the porch and the little girl let me sit down as the grownups started jawing again. Her hand was warm and clammy but I didn't mind her touching me, which kind of surprised me. No one has touched me for over three decades, apart from Dr Reynolds once, and then, I've got to admit, I bit him for his pains. She didn't ask me to speak, which I appreciated, but after a while she took me back inside the house and led me once more to the room where Gem was lying in his cot. She said I could touch him if I liked, because he was asleep, but it was strange touching another person. I patted his head, but she could see that I was unused to this sort of thing. Then she let me go, but as I passed her father he said something to me. I didn't note what it was. Some people need to talk all the time; others don't feel the same need. I guess I'm one of them.

LOOK MA

The strangest thing. He musta thought I was talking about my hooks when I said that the kids had done that to me. I wasn't, of course, I was talking about my general state. Round that time I was in what you might consider a poor condition. Nowheres to live but motel rooms on the edge of whatever town I was at; same clothes for weeks on end; just my polaroid and me trudging round the neighbourhoods, getting barked at by dogs, laughed at by kids and mostly ignored by housewives. Times I'd be walking up a person's drive and I could see them through their lounge windows, but they'd duck behind a door, pretend no one was in. This guy I'm talking about looked like he was going to be one of them too. I could see he was looking out at me for a few moments before he decided to answer the door, but answer he did. As I said, the strangest thing.

You see, times had got hard and I'd had to pawn my watch, a good one that Martha'd bought me for my twenty fifth, and I was more than a mite dissatisfied with what the old guy was prepared to give me for it. I pointed to the Polaroid on the shelf behind him and said, "We'll call it a deal if you'll throw that old thing in too." The guy looked at the camera a while and sighed before taking it down. He turned it over in his hands as if it were something precious, but then he put it down on the counter in front of me.

"Aint much call for 'em these days," he said. "They was all the rage when they first come out, but everyone's gone back to their SLRs, I guess."

I didn't rightly understand what that meant, but I had a kind of idea I could do something with the Polaroid, if it was working anyways. It was right about then that I come up with the idea to go round offering to take pictures of people's houses for them. It'd keep me moving, I thought, and I was guessing my handicap wouldn't prevent me taking the photographs. There's not much to it after all.

And there ain't too much to it. You run off a couple snaps and show them. You tell the person they can have them a photograph right there and then, or they can have an enlargement the next day or so. Surprising how some folks look real intent at the picture, like they'd never seen their own house before. I guess because you're making out you're an expert photographer, that's what they believe you are. It can get kinda tedious work when no one wants to buy though. You get to a point where you're happy to make enough to cover motel expenses for the night and just content yourself that at least you've spoken to another human being that day, or traded a few words on a porch for a while anyway.

It looked like being one of those slow days this time I rang the guy's doorbell. It was hot and sticky out, one of those June days when everyone's too tired to work, if they've got a job, and too tired to do anything round the house if they're a stay-at-home. I'd decided, as soon as I saw it was a man who was going to answer the door, that I may as well just ask for a glass of water, get to sit down for a few minutes if I could.

Lots of folks look at my steel hooks. They can't help it. I don't tell them about the accident because it was years ago now and I'm not looking for sympathy or anything. They want to know how I manage, is what it is, but when they see me click the shutter on my Polaroid with the side of a hook they get the idea that you do manage. Someone recently was telling me that they'd heard of people writing with their toes because they were born without hands. I even heard of people painting like that too. I don't care about that though. It's not as if I'm intending to be any kind of *artist*.

I could see the guy looking down at where my hands should be as he mumbled to come in. But he was happy to let me sit down and rest my bones, and I was happy that he went off to get me a cup of coffee. I looked around the room while he was pouring the coffee. It wasn't anything much; there was an orange and brown swirly carpet that coulda made you sick if you looked at it too long, a tan imitation leather suite and in one corner a kind of cabinet where I guess he kept a bottle of cheap whiskey and some bottles of cordial. Over the mantel there was a clock with gold painted leaves coming out of it, like it was a picture of the sun that some kid had painted. The time was wrong on it so it musta run out of battery. He didn't have any ornaments or anything. No picture frames neither.

It looked like he was renting the place and I hazarded that he was living on his own because his marriage had broke up. I knew he wouldn't want a photograph of the place if it was just somewhere he was passing through. He didn't answer when I asked him if he was married or not, he just asked me something stupid about who I worked with. I told him I worked on my own. It went quiet for a while, until I ventured that I knew what it was like for him. He seemed a tad resentful at me saying that and he quickly changed the subject. He started to talk about me photographing him. I said, "Houses are what I shoot, not people," but he insisted on me taking one of him in the kitchen, one in the living room, one in his bedroom even.

I took over a dozen shots in all. The last two he made me go outside into the street and photograph him standing on his own roof yelling into the middle distance. He paid for ten of the pictures and I decided to let that be my last call of the day. I must have slipped the remaining photos in my inside pocket because when I got back to my room at the Motel 6 one of them fell on the floor when I threw my jacket on the bed. I picked it up, thinking to throw it in the litter basket, but then I noticed something. It was a close-up of the man staring insolently into the camera. But it wasn't the expression on the guy's face that caught my attention; it was the piece of lint on his sleeve of his jacket. I knew this could only mean one thing, that he'd slept in his clothes. It's a free country but I also knew that he was a smoker. I'd seen a big decorative dish on a counter in the kitchen that he clearly used as an ashtray and anyways the house smelled of stale cigarettes. Obviously I know what this means because of what happened to me. I almost felt like catching a bus back to his place and warning him, but people don't want to listen to other people's dramas, do they?

149

It was ten years ago, my drama, and I guess you could tell it in all sorts of different ways. From my ex-wife's point of view it would be a story of how she narrowly escaped burning to death in her own home. She'd be the central character, of course, and it would be a tale of how she sacrificed her chances of a career by falling foolishly in love with a man who drank too much and never cared for her or her kids enough. In this version of things she'd only narrowly escape disaster by being strong enough to leave her nogood husband and meet a new man who'd recognise her strength and the power of the love she had to give. Or from Tom and Millie's point of view it'd be a story of discontented, dysfunctional family life with two feckless parents who could only argue and break things. They'd be perpetually half drunk and instead of providing stability, nourishment and encouragement, they'd veer wildly between forgetting to do any food shopping and treating the family to expensive takeaway meals they couldn't afford. In this version they'd quit school and get jobs rather than go to college, because they'd just have to get away from their selfish mother and her new man. And they'd try hard not to ever think about their crippled father who'd nearly died in a house fire.

But how do you tell a story anyway? From my own point of view what happened isn't really a story. A proper story has some sense of direction, a character doing stuff because he *has* to, and it's got action that means something, leads somewhere. Nothing meant very much to me and not just because I drank too much; it wouldn't have meant anything if I'd been stone sober all day every day. After the accident I admit tried to understand what had happened through cause and effect. Martha had left again after a screaming row. We'd both been hitting the tequila pretty hard that night and it coulda been different: she might have screamed off down the highway, totalled the Maverick and I would have been hauled off the couch by a patrolman to identify my dead wife. She got to where she was going without incident, however. And it was her visiting me in hospital the next day. I actually could have died. These things happen, and it's not *because* of anything.

I bet people who lose limbs in battle, or lose an eye, or get their ear chopped off, stuff like that, try to trace it all back to where events started. Try to understand the logic. There is no logic. A guy I knew in Indiana once was beaten and stabbed to death with the broken end of his own walking cane. Now how do you make any sense of that? He was drinking in a bar in a dump called South Bend and he got into an argument with a couple of fellows. He'd said something to the first guy, who was in a wheelchair, and it rumbled on for a while. Then the guy in the wheelchair said something real quietly and Clyde, the guy I'm talking about, leaned down to catch what he'd said. I wasn't there ,but I gather what happened was this: the wheelchair guy, and get this, he didn't have hands or legs, grabbed him round the neck in the crook of his elbow and started beating on him with the stump of his other arm. Then he shouted to his drinking partner to beat on him too. It was a frenzy of senselessness. Clyde's metal cane broke in the melee and he got stabbed with the splintered end. Just to make sure they drove him down to the river and dumped him in the water in some plastic sheeting.

If he'd had a wife or kids, I don't know if he did or not, I guess they'd have tried to understand it all. They'd have blamed the drink, or the dangerous area of town he'd gone to, or admitted that their husband or father had always been unkind to people with disabilities, or some stuff like that. Truth is, they would have turned away to get on with their own lives though, like the family in that poem they made us read in high school. I can't rightly recall the name of the poem but it was about a woodchopper in Vermont. I thought at the time, when Mr Atkinson was reading us the poem in the slow drawl he had, it was just kind of a warning to us to take care when we were sawing or chopping up kindling. Now I think now it's more to do with life's uncertainties. Or perhaps I mean the certainty of death. I'm not sure I even know what I mean.

As I say, my own little drama happened a decade ago. I was drunk. I fell asleep while I was smoking. The house caught fire and I mighta died just like that, but I didn't. I woke to see flames licking up the curtains. The couch had caught fire but it didn't feel like it was the heat that roused me. I think it was more like a sound that suddenly had me sitting bolt upright staring at the living room, my world, on fire. I must have froze for a minute, trying to comprehend what was going on. I know I didn't try to do anything; I didn't shout, I just ran out into the street. And this is where you can say that hazard has its accuracies. It was two o'clock in the morning and the neighbourhood would normally have been silent and completely empty, but on this one occasion a car was tearing down the street being chased by the police. It swerved straight into me. I could have been run over and that would have been that, but luck had one more throw of the dice for me. I was crushed up against the wall and my hands were pinned under the upturned chassis. Or I thought so anyway. When the truck they got finally dragged the car off of me I could see one hand's still on the sidewalk, completely severed from my wrist. My other hand was kinda hanging by some tendons or sinews, or whatever joins stuff together in a body. It was a Ford Pinto that hit me: the worst car they ever made. Buckled and tore up at the slightest collision, they did. This one did anyways. A piece of fender sheared off one hand and near enough sliced the other one clean off too. They couldn't save it anyway. And I didn't get no compensation from Ford. It was a criminal driving the vehicle and there was no such thing as victim compensation.

I could have died in a fire. I could have subsequently been killed in a car wreck. Destiny had other things in store for me though. And that's alright with me. Since I got fitted with these metal hooks I've found a way of making some kind of living. And you see folks worse off than you. Like the guy I'm telling you about, a person who is so desperate that he'll pay good money to have someone like me take photographs of him in all his misery. Photographs of him rummaging around in the net he's got over his chimney to find some pebbles and rocks that a kid's thrown up there, so's he can throw them into the street. He ain't house cleaning here either; he's filled with rage at the world, at the wife and kids who've left him, at the factory that's closed down and made him redundant, at the neighbours who've got newer automobiles or whatnot. But maybe that's not it either. Like I said, I don't know what's a story and what's just a picture, or whether a picture tells more of a story than a whole story does. It was just the strangest thing though.

COLD CASE

Establishing the truth is not as straightforward as it may seem. Admittedly, as I sit here in my armchair sipping on a good sherry, smoking a fine cheroot, I may appear somewhat smug, a professional man at the forefront of his chosen field, enjoying the rewards of his endeavours. But I would not wish to appear complacent. It is actually true that some cases baffled me, and thus I fear the truth still does its best to elude me. The case of Elizabeth S is a good example. It was not even that it was a particularly difficult case to unravel, if it were simply to be the manner and cause of her death that were to be ascertained. As to this, I have my firm convictions about what happened, but there are other mysteries and they are considerably more difficult to explain. Ah, those artists have a way of throwing shadows over everything, so that you can't quite see what is there and what is not, if you follow my meaning.

I want to start at the beginning, but whose beginning is the first question. For me, it was when Clara Siddall requested my help in trying to resolve some matters that were troubling her regarding her sister. For Clara herself it was, I suppose, when her sister first moved in with Mr Rossetti. But where did it all start for Lizzie? In Hatton Garden the year Sir Robert Peel had his bright idea to set up the metropolitan police at Scotland Yard? Actually, I find coincidences rather disturbing, so I find it a trifle unsettling that this was also the same year that a Danish gentleman wrote about the strange death of the rector of Veilbye, and henceforth it seems that everyone wants to read about a good mystery, but I should say more about that in due course of time. Forgive my digression. I was pondering whether Lizzie's story actually started with her arrival on earth, but it might be better to argue that it truly commenced nearly twenty years later, when Lizzie was working at Mrs Tozer's, and in walks old Deverell.

I can picture her sitting in a corner with a needle in her hand when a fine gentleman causes the shop doorbell to tinkle and Mrs Tozer's heart to go all-a-fluster. That would be the opening scene if one of those gentleman novelists were to set about telling the story, I imagine. Slushy snow outside on the pavements, a urchin bowling a wheel with a stick down the thoroughfare, the smell of kidneys grilling in a iron griddlepan wafting through a window. But it wasn't Christmastide. It wasn't even December. It was, I am fairly confident, late February when Mr Deverell walked through that door and clapped eyes on the most astonishing radiant face he had ever seen. It was, by all accounts, a face of great beauty and of a refinement unusual even in ladies of the highest birth, let alone what you would expect to encounter in the daughter of a mere cutler. But there was more to it than that. The pale and delicate features of this distinguished physiognomy were surrounded by a cloud of red hair that seemed more like something alive and moving, like a kind of coppery waterfall, than a mere head of hair.

People have different attitudes and predispositions towards this hair colouring. For many ordinary folk it is a mark of Celtic origins and I suppose favouring or disfavouring the characteristic of bright red hair depends on whether you have some attachment to the Hibernian races or not. For some other folk there may be a kind of superstition borne out of an awareness that Judas Iscariot had a carroty mop of hair, or that the devil himself is partial to redness. Still others may regret their own dusty brown locks and yearn for the sensational quality of the crowning glory which marked out Elizabeth Siddall.

I suppose it was the strangest thing for a man who was only looking to buy some silk for his hat band, to discover this young woman who would become muse, poet, artist, figure of mystery and appeal to a whole generation. Doubtless he would have had no difficulty finding a model for the Shakespearian scene he was painting anyway. All he would have had to do was take a constitutional in Lambeth or Bow and there would be plenty of young girls walking up and down the lanes there. And nary a one of them would object to donning a fine costume and sitting in a studio for a few hours out of the cold and the smog, you can be sure. A man like Deverell wouldn't normally go to a milliner's to find his models,

I daresay. But that's pretty well what happened. You've got to admit, it does look like the beginning of a story of love and intrigue, don't it?

But I should introduce myself before I go a-rambling off into the metaphysicals of hats and coats and Shakespearian costumes. I am Bucket. I have a certain fame of my own, courtesy of one of the gentleman novelists I alluded to a moment ago. But I am a different man from what you may read of. I am plain spoken, as may well be evident, and I have a certain short shrift kind of a way with them that are determined to hinder, rather than help with my enquiries, that's true too. But there's few that know me that wouldn't argue that I'm capable of seeing that life is a touch more problematical than your average detective is prepared to concede. If you want to picture what I look like, I could try and help you, but what am I to say? A middling sort of man with greying salt and pepper hair and a brownish moustache. An oldish man in a long overcoat. A man with no great distinguishing features. A man you'd pass in the street without notice because there's no singularity about him. It suits me to be so, I have to say. Though in my line of work you might expect a certain degree of subterfuge, I have not needed to wear disguises so very much, because a man without particularities is always in disguise. You'll have to imagine me as you will then. But you can paint on whatever blank, bluff face you have in your mind's eye a pair of steely blue eyes, if you wish. That would not veer too far from the truth.

I'd been working at Scotland Yard about fifteen year when the Tulkinghorn business took my interest. And, if it's not too immodest of me to say it, I was an important figure in the metropolitan force at that time. That was seventeen years ago. Sad enough to say, I have years on my back eight and fifty now, if you'll permit me a modest peregrination into the world and the words of the immortal bard, and these days I content myself with a sort of consulting detective position. This means I can choose which cases I look into, but it does also mean I miss the cut and thrust of regular police work. Nevertheless, I still have access to records and documents at the Yard and I still have a good number of allies and friends there too, I should say. Anyway, it's because I do have a certain freedom that I found myself with time enough and interest enough to get involved in the Lizzie Siddall business.

Miss Clara Siddall contacted me by letter, saying that she could not quite eliminate doubts she had about the manner and cause of her sister's unfortunate death eight years previously. Eight years is a long time, but I could well enough apprehend that one may harbour doubts and queries about the premature loss of a loved one for easily that long, ay, and a good while longer. But it was, if I'm candid, the fact that I had heard of Elizabeth Siddall's decease at the time, and wondered myself how events had taken the sad turn that they had, that excited my interest. Thus I was only too ready to meet Miss Clara and discuss the matter.

We arranged a rencontre at a coffee shop in Greenwich and, though I had never seen her face before, I instantly knew that the tall, slender figure in the grey topcoat who hurried into the shop five minutes late was Lizzie Siddall's sister. She did not have her sister's mane of red hair, but she had the same oval grey eyes and rather long aquiline nose. She also had a languorous manner of speech which somehow chimed with the image I had of Lizzie's whole placid, deliquescent nature. I have to admit though that the image I had at the time of the subject of my enquiries was probably largely drawn from her portraiture. My subsequent investigations have suggested that she may well have had a rather more fiery demeanour.

I got up to greet Miss Clara Siddall and I directed her to the window table that I had occupied, for I'd had a mind to watch as people passed by outside. She shook my hand limply without removing her kid glove and accepted my offer of a hot drink, for it was a chilly day and she seemed exhausted, as if from a long walk. Then, when she was settled in her seat and had a hot chocolate before her, she started to tell me of the fears she had had for her sister's sanity during the months preceding her death, although she admitted that she had told the coroner's inquest that Lizzie had demonstrated a lightness and good humour in the days immediately before the tragedy. There was an incongruity here which I could not fail to note, but I said nothing and let her continue. She said that she did not really suspected foul play, but something that had happened more recently had roused her to want to know more about the

156

events of February 1862. This recent set of events was singular enough for me to assure her that I would look into the case and report my findings as soon as ever I could.

Obviously my first step was to investigate the court records. The coroner was happy enough to record her death as accidental. Misadventure is the new-fangled term for it but I don't like that word, it's imprecise. At the inquest Mr Rossetti said poor Lizzie was distraught and invariably of a nervous disposition, so she relied on laudanum to get a night's sleep. The housekeeper, Mrs Birrell, confirmed that she'd seen the phial of laudanum beneath Miss Siddall's pillow. (I suppose I should use the young woman's married name here because she was referred to as Mrs Rossetti at the inquest, but I'll adhere to Lizzie Siddall, because that's what history seems to want to remember her as). Strangely though, the maid mentioned that the 'little bottle', as she termed it, was always kept on the rosewood chiffonier in Miss Siddall's bedchamber. Staff can be notoriously unreliable when it comes to domestic details though, which is surprising when you consider that such things are the apparatus of their very existence. Notwithstanding, no one denies that she had a blue glass bottle with a potion made of opium and brandy diluted in a little water, and no one asserts anything other than that it was the consumption of this admixture that caused her demise. What was of concern to the coroner's examination was, of course, the identity of the person who dealt out the fateful dose. Was it a second party and therefore a case of murder, or manslaughter at least? Or was it by her own hand, which would adumbrate the possibility of suicide, but might also be regarded as a case of misadventure?

Miss Clara had asked me to scrutinise the records and speak to those people who were closest to her sister, in order to determine if there was indeed something underhand about the tragic death. But it was in looking into the matter of her decease that I uncovered another set of mysteries. And there are a number of them. I will try to tell you about each of these in the plainest terms, but it is a problem, I have to concede.

First, however, the death of the young woman. As she had told me at the coffee shop, Clara informed the coroner that she was of the view that Lizzie was in good spirits when she had seen her on the previous Saturday, three days before her passing, which suggests that suicide was unlikely. Mrs Birrell also stated that Mrs Rossetti, as she called her throughout the inquest, was in a good mood during the afternoon of Monday February 9th. Only when she attended her mistress's chamber at eleven thirty that night was she made aware that there was anything untoward. Of course, it was Mr Rossetti who summoned her to the bedroom at that time. She did state that she had passed the bedroom door half an hour earlier and all was quiet at that time. I am happy to conclude that Sarah Birrell had no motive for committing a heinous crime against her mistress. Lizzie was of an inconsistent disposition and prone to fits of irrational behaviour, but she was not a martinet to her staff. In addition Sarah Birrell is an honest soul, not to mention a somewhat comely matron, whom I could not suspect of any wrongdoing.

The only other suspect, if one were to pursue the notion that a crime had been committed, was of course her husband. Mr Rossetti was not always faithful to Lizzie, of that we can be sure. By virtue of his profession he spent a lot of time with beautiful young models, and to some men that might be an irresistible temptation to stray. I have to say that I am forced to question the moral fibre and motivations of such men as choose the artistic way of life, but let that be. But Rossetti does not seem to have hated his wife, or even harboured the sort of resentment that might make him even think of staging an accidental overdose, or worse, a suicide. He dined with his wife at a friend's house, escorted the lady home and then went out again for a period of about three hours. I cannot suppose that he forced her to imbibe an inproportionate dose of laudanum and then blithely left the house, for that would not be a murderous husband's way. No, he may have wanted to relieve himself of her too nervous company, but I'm sure he did nothing to engineer a permanent removal.

So, murder was not a likely reason for her death. In these matters you have to consider motive as well as opportunity, but the usual motives are absent. She was not independently wealthy; she had no jealous rival; there was no dark secret from her past that someone

158

needed to conceal. Indeed, the secrets and mysteries surrounding Lizzie Siddall's case all pertain more to events subsequent to her demise, but once again I am leaping forward in my tale. The bath, the hair, the poems, her age, the depression, the anomaly of whether she is to be regarded as protagonist or victim; all of these are shrouded by uncertainties, but I shall come to each of these in due course.

Having quickly disposed of the notion that she was murdered, I turned my attention to the possibility that Lizzie had after all taken her own life. She had been subjected to the horrors of death early in life, at the tender age of eight years in fact, when a famous trial took place at the Old Bailey and the Siddalls' landlord, James Greenacre, was found guilty of murdering his wife, Hannah. He had killed her as a consequence of a dispute over whether they should emigrate to Australia, which seems odd enough in itself, then he had deposited the dismembered body in Regent's Canal. Her head was found floating in the murky waters there by an officer from Marylebone. I'm not sure if it's fanciful or not, but you could think that this image of the dead woman in the water may have persisted in Lizzie Siddall's consciousness throughout her brief life. It's certainly an image which attaches itself indelibly to her own history, though most people would want to believe that it is the artistic vision of Millais and not the macabre doings of Greenacre that define poor Lizzie.

It was fifteen years after the Greenacre case that Lizzie posed for John Everett Millais. Her pale complexion, her long birdlike nose, and her slender, graceful form seemed perfect for his portrayal of Ophelia, that most tragic of Shakespeare's heroines. He insisted on getting every detail right, of course, for he was a painter who believed in veracity as well as classical precision, or so I am told by those who know about such things. To this end he spent a considerable amount of time, and a very large sum of money, obtaining a fine old dress, embroidered in a delicate silver filigree. Mr Parson, the haberdasher who sold the dress to Millais, remembers the garment to this day. "Four pound he paid me for it," he told me proudly, when I visited his grimy little emporium in Southwark, "Though it was a work of art. I daresay it may have been worn by some great lady too, it were that old."

The artist also insisted that his model be immersed in actual water for his composition, though it might have been kinder of him to paint her in a prone position and add the effect of the rippling water after, to my way of thinking. He had her lie in a metal bathtub raised from the floor, in order that oil lamps be placed beneath it. He intended to keep the water at least tepid, it seems, for Miss Siddall's comfort. He failed to observe that the lamps ran out of fuel, however, so long was he in his work. The result was that Lizzie caught a severe cold and fell quite ill. Her father insisted that Millais pay all the medical bills incurred by his negligence, but it is to be supposed that they were a small price for the artist to pay, compared to the recognition that his work received when it was displayed at the Royal Academy. But one may wonder what price was paid by his model, for this seems to be the beginning of a long period of illness and distraction that she suffered over the next ten years.

I discovered from a conversation I had with Sarah Birrell that Lizzie removed to Hastings a couple of years after, in order to recuperate from one of these bouts of ill health, and her time in France during the summer of the following year was also devoted to recovering from another attack of nervous depression. It is a matter of record that she met the poet Robert Browning in that metropolis but it is also clear that the meeting did not go well. In late summer she removed from Paris to Nice because the doctors told her that the sun and the sea waters would help her condition. This time abroad I could not investigate more fully, however, because I did not have the necessary means to fund a trip to France. Anyway I decided that my time would be better spent retracing Lizzie's footsteps back in England, where she returned in late 1855.

Lizzie and Rossetti had set up house in Blackfriars, at 14 Chatham Place, to be exact, and they were due to marry in the summer of 1856, but for reasons that he was not prepared to go into on the sole occasion I was able to meet with him, Rossetti reneged on his proposal. Understandably, Lizzie was intensely distraught at her fiancé's sudden intransigence and she fled from the house to Bath in shame and mortification. Now I do not know Bath well, but I have read Miss Austen's accounts of the viperous gossiping of the ladies in that city, certainly as it was thirty or forty years earlier anyway, and to my mind it was not the sort of place that would have provided much comfort to a jilted young woman of reputedly nervous disposition. Perhaps it was just as well, therefore, that Rossetti followed her there and persuaded her to return to London. He would not tell me what passed between them, what promises may have been made or what threats issued at that time, but Lizzie did not stay long back in the metropolis. She left for Matlock, in Derbyshire, the following spring. Now here is the fountainhead of one of the mysteries of Lizzie's last few years: did she go to Derbyshire, and subsequently to Yorkshire, to further her artistic ambitions, or was she seeking to resolve a family dispute?

Lizzie's father was, as I have said, a cutler by trade. That might suggest some connection with Sheffield, where knives are the town's main industry, as everyone knows, and this is where she went after a short time in Matlock. But Mr Siddall spent an inordinate amount of time pursuing a family concern rather than plying his own trade. It is a strange coincidence, though I do not like such things, as I have already indicated, but the particular family matter that so absorbed Siddall was the question of an inheritance, the same concern that was at the core of the Tulkinghorn affair that brought me to some prominence, and that therefore led Clara Siddall to my door all these years later. In Siddall's case the disputed property was one New Hall in Hope, in Derbyshire. Nothing ever came of the claim he made on the property, unfortunately, and the discovery that nothing ever would come of it may have been what drove Lizzie a step further to her own destruction. There was to be no Hope, you might say, and old Siddall's folly could be likened to that of the father of that poor girl that Mrs T, my former housekeeper, told me about once. That is a story that deserves to be told, but I digress again.

The time Lizzie spent in the North of England was not, however, solely spent chasing the shadow of an inheritance. Indeed, it is to be doubted whether she was very much concerned about money, for she had a generous patron in the esteemed Mr Ruskin, and had sold pictures and designs enough to regard herself as financially independent by this time. I dutifully read some of the poems she published during these years too, though I must admit that they do not stir me like the verse of Mr

Browning or Lord Tennyson. Perhaps that is because I am a man, and more affected by manly subjects, though Lord Tennyson did write about a mad woman locked away in a castle, or grange perhaps it was, and to my mind there's something about the lass in that poem that echoes the rather morbid young lady Miss Siddall describes in her verse, looking for death and wandering around the woods and so forth. I'm not sure if one can get close to what may be taking place within a writer's mind by reading ballads, however. Who is to say a writer is telling the truth when he tells a story?

She only wrote a handful of poems, as far as I can ascertain, for she was more determined to succeed as a painter, and that is the reason that Clara and Mr Rossetti gave me for her travelling to Yorkshire and Derbyshire. Neither of those persons said anything about the Hope business, but I have it on the authority of a neighbour of Mr Siddall's in Southwark that she may have been trying to kill a brace of birds with the one stone. Clearly the air in the North of England did not agree with her, however, for she had to return to London in 1858. Mr Rossetti had been conducting some relations with another young lady, a Miss Ann Miller, but I am persuaded to believe that he decided to end that business and devote his attentions entirely to Lizzie. Perhaps he grew tired of travelling down to Derbyshire to sit at her sick bed, or perhaps he genuinely believed she might recover in the London air.

I visited the painter Madox Brown at his rooms in Kentish Town, having been led to understand that he knew a good deal about Rossetti's circle, though he did not class himself as one of the brethren. He was a sensitive looking man who wore his greying hair with a youthful abandon and who eschewed a moustache. He looked to me as if he might have wanted to be born a woman, but he was a bluff enough cove once we began to talk. He was initially coy about discussing the Siddall affair, but once I told him my motives were to put the sister's mind at ease he seemed prepared to divulge what he knew. He told me he felt that Rossetti had had a premonition that Lizzie would not be long for this world and it was almost certainly an act of honour and loyalty to reinstate Lizzie in Chatham Place for as long as she might survive.

Lizzie did survive this illness, of course. Two years later she and Rossetti were finally married and she almost immediately conceived a child. Whether Rossetti had decided to marry her after all as some act of contrition, or because he did not expect her to live any great length of time is a moot point. I have not found any evidence that he grieved the loss of his stillborn daughter a year later, however. Having said that, it is certain that he was consumed with grief at his wife's death. He may or may not have known that she was once more with child, for her condition was not remarked upon at her inquest, clearly for reasons of delicacy.

So, what are we to understand? Lizzie Siddall was a working class girl who became a minor poet and an artist of sorts but who was foiled in the more expected feminine ambitions of a happy marriage and children? Lizzie Siddall was an ingénue who was swept up and away by a seductive crew of Pre-Raphaelite bacchanalians and inevitably tumbled into a life of opium addiction and early death? She was objectified, frozen (literally, in Millais' bath tub) and reduced to a two dimensional life? Was Lizzie Siddall a cipher, a symbol, a canvas on which the romantics among us like to paint whatever motif of tragedy or triumph we wish? Was she, god bless us, a reincarnation of her Danish forebear Ophelia? In any of these lights, she may live forever. One thing is sure. She did not physically endure in the grave. She was not still young, beautiful and untouched by the ravages of the worms when Rossetti's men exhumed the body last year. Whatever they say, I cannot believe this. I said at the outset I am a bluff man, but not incapable of understanding that life is a mysterious business, but I cannot be moved to believe this account.

I mentioned that Rossetti was consumed by grief at Lizzie's death. One act suggests that this was the case; the fact that he buried the only manuscript he had of his poems in poor Lizzie's coffin. This act has to be interpreted as the gesture of a man totally stricken by the loss of his wife. Or, you might say, if you were more of a sceptical bent, as the act of a man who likes to perform great gestures. He buried the poems in the great nest of Lizzie's untamed red hair. When Rossetti's friend William Howell and his men dug up the grave they claimed that Lizzie's face was pure, virginal, untouched by mortality. Her hair, always long and curling down in rich red waves, had continued to grow, they later said, and now reached her hips. The poems were there of course, but the paper, albeit protected by a calfskin covering, had become soiled after seven years in the deep earth. But, according to Rossetti, they were capable of restoration. He told me his doctor friend Francis Hutchinson disinfected and dried the pages and returned them so that they could after all see the light of day in the form of a book of verses. Madox Brown, on the other hand, told me he saw the manuscript, and it was filled with worm holes.

And one other thing: Elizabeth Siddall's hair was not her own. She suffered from a very severe form of alopecia and had worn a wig since she was seventeen.

As to Mr Rossetti, he is rather a melancholic character to this day, though he amuses himself with maintaining a sort of menagerie of animals in the grounds of his house. He has monkeys, armadillos, gazelles, peacocks, a kangaroo, a wombat, and a large black bull, all of which he allows to roam his gardens. I hear he pines for an elephant, but that may just be another story.

BOB & CO

Yes, they are all here at the hospital, that bordello of original sin and concupiscence. Frankie and J.P., the professor and the man in the long black coat, Sara and Isis, Bob, Ira and Hattie (poor woman since slain by a cane), that girl with the five inch smile, Tiny Montgomery, Johanna and Louise, Reuben and Davey Moore, Maggie and little Sadie, Diamond Joe and Big Jim; Lily, Rose, the whiskey-soaked judge and sweet Marie and Arthur McBride, the whole shebang. Donald White is here, bracing his neck muscles; Hollis Brown with his sad face; Ruby and Henry Porter feeling raw; Curtis and Delia; Denise and Angelina; face after face distorted by time and art and too much high living.

They are just a bunch of yahoos all looking for meaning but pushing their own agendas; all with their own stories, but they're just fragments that echo fragments of other stories. They're faceless extras. They think they're on a journey and every one of them thinks he's the central protagonist but it's only a roundabout and they're all bit parts, even me, the man in the macintosh.

Yes, I'm sitting here nursing my drink. I've sat with counts and soldiers, citizens and patriots, ranchers and loggers, courtiers and gravediggers. I watch over the rim of my libation as they circle and collide, like ants or bumper cars, not seeing that history is no arrow, but a boomerang sweeping around the world, a crazy comet on a long and pointless parabola. Some of them try to make their mark, plant a heavy footprint in the ground or scratch their name in the sand. Some sing of their sadness or joy and dream of their days in Tangiers or Morocco, their time in the North or the West, yearn for their lost loves as they gaze from a window opened wide. Most of them get drunk, argue and proselytise, gossip and snipe, write postcards that hurt.

But who am I? Call me Bob. Bob in the corner, if you will. I've spent my unnameable days in bars and whorehouses but I've also whiled away the hours in galleries and sad cafes. I've been to London and I've been to gay Paree; I've gone down to the levee and to school in Germany. In my cockle hat, with dust on my long black coat, I've walked the streets of Oxford town and Mobile, chewing on a Danish and thinking about the law. At Davy Byrne's I fed that old black dog; another time I crossed the street to get away from the mangy old thing, all the time talking in a monologue that's full of semi colons and empty of sense. In that other bar I saw a reflection of myself in the reverend face of Charles Malone, fresh back from Ithica, and I saw a man feeding the gulls in the big wide river but I didn't pay much mind because all the while I was dreaming of sleeping in Rosie's bed. I drew a face on a napkin in a diner in Boston but I was thinking of someone else's face, Martha's face in fact. Let the day turn to night, my dear Marion, I said.

It doesn't matter if I'm here in this waiting room, upstairs in the rooms with the beds, or in some far off saloon, I'm invisible anyway. All you can see is the throng of expression-filled faces, the eager, the blissful, the crazy, the serious, the unhappy and the merely discontented. Faces framed to fill the hours; faces tagged by someone else. But these are the walk-ons, the people at the back of the auditorium just there to stop the place looking empty. Presently in will come the characters: the sad eyed lady dreaming of her flowers; the boy with the blistered tongue, the black man with one trouser leg stitched up to his thigh; the mournful lady in the calico dress; the wrinkled old navel-gazing priest; the haughty Frenchman with his aristocratic nose in the air; the man with no name who wears a jacket with sleeves that come down way too far; that stunning redhead with the impassive eyes; the man who claimed to be the brother of the saviour of the nation; the man with one eye and a muleskinner's hat; the pale faced loner; and of course, hobbling in at the rear, the bibulous Mrs T, still in her apron, still gabbing and gossiping and dying for a drink.

They're all playing parts, of course. One is the uncle from a Moliere drama; another is the romantic lead; a third is the mysterious stranger who comes to the door to bring the news that lives are going to change. The ragamuffin lad is the leader of the chorus line in a musical; the courtier with the bells on his shoes is the hero's best friend. The ashen faced gent is the bogeyman from the frightfest. You can recognise them from the movies they've been in or are yet to be in. They form a mille-feuille of humanity but although it may be satisfying to have lots of layers, you need room to see the layers, there needs to be light between them to separate out all the threads.

What if, I wonder, sipping at my drink, what if I could summon them to different auditions, to see what other roles they might have played? If they are truly just a repertory company of jobbers we might have seen a slatternly Lizzie puffing at an opium pipe in a dark corner of a shanty bar in Brazil. There, if the camera's loving eye had lingered as it rove the room, we might have seen a couple of card players, one with a poacher's gun slung from the back of his rickety cane chair, and opposite him a disenchanted young man with a soldier's moustache. The camera would pause and we would see that he sat in a wheelchair with a blanket across his knees. We would suspect some subterfuge with the blanket, perhaps a soldier's pistol concealed in its folds. The matron who appears from a room within at first might seem a sturdy woman of some fifty or so years, but her face, as the lens closes in and the studio lights irradiate it in a yellow funnel of romantic possibility, transforms into that of a confident young black woman girl half that age. She wears bright earrings and flashes bright teeth.

Or we might be in a different bar. In a dusty tavern in rural Dorset, say, or a bright shiny bistro in London's West End perhaps. Here, a gaunt, bright eyed man of middle years with a mop of shaggy salt and pepper hair and a hippy leather bracelet is expounding on capitalism, bourgeois values and history in general. He has buttonholed a perky young lad in a jacket of archaic (or is it fashionable?) velveteen and he's telling him of the atrocities committed in the name of religion or political credo by various bodies and regimes. We have all met such men. The boy is struggling to respond from time to time but he is alert to the other patrons, as if expecting to be accosted at any moment.

Into this tavern, or bar, comes a man with one eye. His entrance is noted by sundry of the drinkers there, for he does not wear an eye patch and his face is therefore remarkable for its grotesque appearance. He is supporting himself with an ashplant and murmuring to himself as he inspects his new surroundings with his one good eye. He stares for some minutes at a woman who is occupying a bar stool a few feet away. There is an air of languor about this woman that suggests she is a frequent visitor to this bar. In the finely tapered fingers of one hand a cigarette dangles; her long beige cardigan speaks of nothing but insouciance; a half empty glass of white wine before her is smudged at the rim with lipstick of scarlet. She has a fine head of rich auburn hair, the tresses of which coil down past her shoulders like sleeping snakes. She takes in the newcomer and registers nothing, though her eyes are brazen and fearless. Then she turns to her left, where a man who has just approached the bar is standing a foot or so away, and she bathes him in a cryptic smile worthy of Leonardo.

The man is wearing luminous training shoes that bear a strange inscription. He cannot prevent himself from uttering a sigh as he shares an unbidden instant with this beautiful stranger. The one-eyed old man raps his walking stick on the parquet flooring, as if in bitter reproof. And the sound seems to stir a pale faced young man at the other end of the counter. He has had his head lowered, sipping a soft drink and avoiding eye contact with everyone in the room. Now he seems vexed at the petulance of the man with the walking stick. He says nothing, however. He never speaks, and no one thinks to approach him either, for there is a darkness about the eyes and a grimace about the mouth that do not invite intercourse.

There are two people serving behind the bar: one is a frumpy lady in a floral dress whose fleshy arms are mottled with cellulite. She has a cackle of a laugh when she decides to appear jocular, but a good deal of the time she prefers to lean against the raised flap of the counter and watch morosely as the people in the bar waste their time and hers in their daily round of hopelessness. She jingles her nine carat gold chain against her wrist or pulls down a bleached blonde curl of her hair to inspect it. She says nothing to her co-worker, the other person waiting to serve. He is a tall young man whom you'd probably suspect to be of antipodean origin, but who is in fact from a small town in Northern France, some

168

unheard of parish in Normandy. He is doubtless a student, supporting himself through a cold English summer by working in this hostelry. He taps his hand against the seam of his jeans and sniffs the air like a dog.

And here is our cast, the whole company, except for two men who now appear from the direction of the rest rooms. One is a man on crutches who makes his way ponderously over to his window seat. He has a heavily lined leather brown face, for he hails from the Caribbean. It is the scowling face of a man disappointed by life's travails. A second man appears in the threshold of the door that leads to the toilets. He pauses, as if still adjusting his clothes, and we see the flash of a chrome hook poking out from his long sleeve. These men are not heroes, they are victims in other people's heroic adventures, but they look like they resent that status.

The bar is quiet. Everyone is waiting for the cry "Action!" But there is no story yet; the actors are waiting for the scriptwriter to turn up. There is some non-diegetic sound, perhaps a contemporary song with lyrics that could turn out to be ironically appropriate; more likely the half-heard strains of a melody suggestive of the mood of expectancy, or reminiscent of other soundtracks of love, or loss, or violent sudden drama. Or perhaps there is a jukebox, if we are, after all, in the London bistro bar. A man in a long dusty coat is standing chiaroscuro against the bright lights of the machine. He is pondering which song to choose from the catalogue of banalities.

We want something to happen and we want it to be real and we want it to be strange. We yearn for the novelty of events beyond our own small compass, where feeding the dog, feeding the machine and feeding our starved imaginations with the daily pulp of TV is a range of experience too narrow to satisfy. We want to believe that such strangeness is possible, but we also want to believe that it will make some sense. The things that happen must happen with a certain inevitability, rather than with the haphazardness that afflicts our own small lives. The actors need to know where they are going, why they act in such fashion, what motivates them so strongly to be so strong, so focused and yes, damn it, so hubristic.

But, like real people in the world beyond the back lot or the studio, these characters are too confused and too complex to act from a single motive. They are not avenging a sister who was raped when she was fifteen; they are not looking for a long lost father who ran away across the seven seas or into the darkest jungle of Congo or Cambodia. They are not society's blameless protectors or guilt ridden and dishevelled drink fuelled divorcees throwing their energies into chasing down wrongdoers. They're not even obsessive outsiders who have stumbled on a government or multinational conspiracy. They have no through line to guide and prompt their every twitch and sarcastic utterance. Their apparel is not selected with care to suggest their fastidiousness, their panache, their abandon. They are wearing what they happened to put on this dull day. They say things like, "Who's running in the 3.30 at Ascot?" or "Did you see old Dennis and his Mrs arguing on the street? A sight for sore eyes it was."

So shall I cry "Action!" or not? Would you relax, for you are tense with that unease that afflicts the unnarratived life, and be content that something at last is going to happen? As soon as somebody speaks, or draws a knife or a gun, or puts down a slim manila envelope on a table, you know that destinies are going to intertwine and unfold in a sequence of events, or scenes, that reveal who you can root for, who dismiss as mere victim, sidekick or temporary love interest. Is it already too late to focus on the man who has entered last, for example, or the woman in the cardigan perhaps? There are too many players in this company, I think you are murmuring to yourself. They may each have a story of some sort, but so does Brian who lives next door – he once met the president – but he doesn't know how to tell his own tale, for it does not reflect his whole life. It's just something that happened when a lot of other things were going on with his family, his job and his feelings about his dead mother. He didn't realise it could be anything more than a moment, an anecdote at best. These strangers in this saloon, they are neighbours, or facebook friends, not real, throbbing personalities whom you could fall in a sort of love with and need. And I mean need in the way, say, that we need music or paintings. Nevertheless, you still may be looking for a face that marks its owner out, the face of a Telemachus if

170

not an Odysseus. A person who is going on a journey and may invite you along.

Someone gets up from a chair. We hear the scrape and squeak of wood on parquet, the clunk of an empty glass put down, the rustle of a coat or a dress. Violins shiver and an oboe sighs. But no. Someone is just going to the toilet. The young man behind the bar – he is dying for a name, so we'll call him Ronaldo for now – moves forward to the counter and picks up a cloth. Is he going to speak? No. He wipes a stain on the good wood and steps back to his sentry post. A voice can be heard faintly from another room, a bar at the rear of this place. Someone is singing. Is it a patriotic ballad or is it a country number filled with the unctuous glue of trailer park tragedy? It's too faint to be heard. It's just diegetic noise. More clumsy realism.

You let your eyes pan around the room in one long crane shot. There's a clock on the wall but it's one of those gimmicky affairs where the hands move in an anti-clockwise motion and it's difficult to read at first. No clues there then; it's not two minutes to the hour or some such tense countdown time. There's a coat stand, but the single item hanging there - a workman's luminous high visibility jacket – is equally unpromising. You doubt that the woman in the cardigan will ease herself from her stool and slip a note into a side pocket, for instance. She is too busy inspecting her makeup now anyway, peering into the mirror of an old fashioned compact she has taken from her expensive brown leather bag. Just past the coat stand is a poster on the wall, a retro view of a coastline bathed in sunlight, with a girl's laughing face in the foreground. Just something from the prop department. There is the door to the rest rooms, marked W.C.'s, but the unnecessary apostrophe, though it stands out to those of a pedantic bent, means nothing.

Your eyes continue their sweep of the bar. The man with the flashy trainers has his back to us now; he is looking up at a wall-mounted television screen, but his eyes do not direct us to anything of significance there. A commercial for home insurance is playing on mute. Just this side of the woman with the compact is the one-eyed man. He has one hand resting on a bar stool against which he has propped his walking cane. He is scowling at the glass tumbler he has in his right hand, as if it is not something he has ordered, but a medicine he has been compelled to imbibe. At the table nearby are the ageing hippy and the anxious lad. They are not talking anymore; in fact it is plain to see now that they are not together, for the younger man is reading a newspaper and the shaggy haired man is staring up at the ceiling.

You realise. They are just parts. They do not make a whole. In fact they conspire to make a hole. The little half-dramas they act out are just that, gaps sewn around with intricate seaming and delicate filigree, but signifying nothing. They are all missing something too: an eye, an ear, a tongue, a finger, a leg, their own hair. Or perhaps what they are missing is not so obvious: it is something hidden or internal. What they lack is more like a means to connect, for in this world of strands they are just stray fibres.

In a way you are glad.

But wait ...

Someone is shouting in the bar at the rear. It is a demented cry like that of a prisoner who hears the footsteps of someone coming to unlock his cell. But what is that almost unintelligible sound? What is the voice saying? The sound grows louder, the voice becomes clearer. A man bursts into the room, his hair an x-ray of craziness, his face beaded in perspiration, his voice, as he almost weeps the utterance, cracking in pain.

"Action!" I cry.

And you put down the book.

Acknowledgements

I have made lots of mistakes in this book, but some of them are deliberate, I swear. Any work of fiction is in part a product of memory and memories are faulty, so it seemed right to have characters offering flawed and inaccurate accounts of themselves from time to time. And it is fun to twist history, as I am sure a great number of politicians would attest.

To those who pointed out the inaccuracies in my multiple drafts of this book I am grateful for their diligent reading. Jamie and Ainsley were particularly diligent, and patient when I argued back. Thank you both for that and for a whole lot else, of course. My wife Rachel was too kind to point out glitches but I have a huge debt of gratitude for her support and encouragement. Indeed, if it were not for her insistence that there was something special about this book, it might never have seen the light of the day. Thanks again for that and for everything that is good in my life.

My publisher Chris Jones has been another patient and reassuring soul and I would like to thank the indomitable Sarla Langdon for her advice and help.